In The
Secret
Hours

Marilyn Jaye Lewis

First Magic Carpet Inc. edition August 2003

Published in 2003

Manufactured in the United States of America
Published by Magic Carpet Books

Magic Carpet Books
PO Box 473
New Milford, CT 06776

Library of Congress Cataloging in Publication Date

In The Secret Hours by Marylin Jaye Lewis
ISBN 0-9726339-4-4

Cover Design: P. Ruggieri

For Mike

Chapter One

Evie Donovan eased open the screen door as quietly as she could. Everywhere the world was peaceful and dark. The summer night welcomed her at last, having kept close her secrets since the night before. She was eager to get moving, to make her escape. All day she'd waited for this, for darkness to come; just like an anxious lover, she'd waited.

As if she knew what that was like, to be anybody's lover.

That was going to change, though, that pathetic predicament. She was going to find a lover, she'd decided, somehow, some way.

But the minute her foot touched the creaking planks of the old wooden porch she knew she wasn't alone. From the corner of her eye she caught the warm glow of a citronella candle burning low at the far end of the veranda, and then the fainter glow of her father's cigarette punctuated the darkness.

"Evie, where you off to this time of night?"

What was he doing out here?

"Hey, daddy," she sighed, her heart sinking over this sudden change of plans. "I just wanted to get some air."

"Those mosquitoes'll eat you alive out there, honey, you know that. Why don't you come sit here by me? The air's better."

Reluctant to disagree with her father, Evie walked the length of the extravagant old porch in silence and sat down next to him.

"I can feel the restlessness in you, Evie, honey. What's the matter with you these days?"

"Nothing, daddy."

"Nothing, daddy," he echoed quietly in mild exasperation. "I wasn't born yesterday, you know."

"I know you weren't," she said just to be saying something, anything at all; Evie's father was suspicious of silence.

"Then tell me what's going on with you, girl?"

"Nothing," she insisted.

"Then where were you off to just now, all alone, at this time of night? And don't think I don't know it's been going on all week," he added. "So you be careful how you answer that. Don't lie to me."

Evie had no intention of lying to her daddy, but she didn't want to tell him the truth, either. It was too personal. She had no choice but to keep silent then, even though she knew it drove him crazy.

As always, her father had drawn the winning hand. How could he have known about this, she wondered. Had he been following her all week? It wasn't possible; most of those nights he hadn't even been home.

Vera, Evie decided. It has to have been Vera; she found out and she told. The two were as thick as thieves.

"What's all the silence about over there, Evie? You trying to think up something good?" He exhaled a final cloud of smoke in the dark and then methodically stubbed out his cigarette.

"No, daddy, there's nothing I need to think up."

"Then what's going on around here? What've you been up to?"

"Nothing, I just like to go out walking. That's all."

"Walking where?"

"Nowhere, just walking. Just… around."

"In the middle of the night?"

"It's not the middle of the night, daddy."

"Well, it's late, regardless," he replied impatiently. "So what's all this secrecy about? Vera says you've been trying to slip in and out all week without anyone knowing you've been gone. Why would you want to do a thing like that, especially at night? It doesn't sound to me like you're going nowhere and doing nothing."

"I'm over twenty-one," Evie said stubbornly. "I can come and go as I please. I don't see why it's got to be anybody else's business."

"Is that right?" her father answered quietly, a hint of menace underscoring his words. "Well, let me tell you something, Evie." He stood up and lifted her firmly by her arm.

"Daddy, don't."

"I don't care how old you are," he went on, undeterred. "You mind how you talk to me – I'm still your daddy."

She squirmed to get her arm free of him as he ushered her toward the porch steps in the dark. "Stop it," she said.

"No," he insisted. "You're in such a hurry to go nowhere and do nothing, I wouldn't want to be accused of holding you up. Excuse me for being concerned about you." Then making a big show of it, he urged her gracelessly down the porch steps. "You go ahead and go now," he told her. Then he went inside, letting the screen door bang closed with a flourish before slamming the front door.

Evie stood at the bottom of the porch steps, dumbfounded. She waited, listening for the heavy click of the front bolt, to hear if he'd go so far as to lock her out, but at least he spared her that insult.

"Jesus Christ," she muttered, not sure if her daddy was still listening; if he wasn't standing just inside, motionless, maybe watching her through the curtains, maybe getting ready to follow her.

When she saw her father's light go on in the window upstairs, she felt a little safer. I think I'm losing my mind, she thought, that's what it is.

Still, she watched and waited. She couldn't help herself. He might trick her; he might come to his window on the sly and spy on her from up there.

"But I am over twenty-one," she reminded herself. "I'm practically twenty-two. This is just crazy. When is he going to realize I'm grown up?"

Not anytime soon. She knew better. Big Joe Donovan was never going to let Evie out of his sight until the perfect suitor had come along to claim her for his bride – whether she wanted to get married or not. And the likelihood of any man striking Big Joe as a perfect suitor for his daughter, and the sole heir to a vast fortune, was slim to say the very least.

At last, she turned her back on the light in her father's window and went off in search of adventure. But it felt different now. It wasn't like it had been all week, where she'd gone off into the dark alone, giddy from the mystery of it, the closeness of the earth's secrets. She'd wander off the meticulously manicured lawn and go in among the wild trees, the night sounds all around her, filling her ears, the peculiar after-dark world of the insects and owls. A bat darting occasionally overhead would startle her, sending a sudden thrill through her belly. Or the way the Spanish moss looked at night, hanging down like clumps of lace, the moon rising fat and full up over the towering oaks, to Evie it was all enchanting. They were the same trees that had stood there since before her great-grandfather had walked the earth or even her great-great-grandfather, whoever those men had been. It seemed as if everyone but Evie's father had been stone cold dead since long before she was born.

The property had been in Evie's family for over two centuries, long before the affluent town of Solisville had sprung up around it. It used to be one of those enormous jaw-dropping plantations isolated on the river road just north of New Orleans. It had thrived on the bloody profits of sugar cane, indigo, and cotton. The house itself had been built entirely by slave labor after the Revolutionary War, a fact that Evie, who had been educated in a private girls' school up north, was secretly ashamed of.

But it wasn't the Donovans who had founded that early empire that had been the curse of untold slaves. It had been a long line of DuMarets who had built it, a feisty and shrewd succession of French businessmen who propagated enormous Catholic families. After an abundant reign spanning over two hundred years, the ancestral line had dwindled down to Evie's mother, Clarice, who had died when Evie was born. She had been the last of the DuMarets. The mansion and the DuMaret land had passed to Clarice's young husband upon her early death, to Joseph Donovan, a broad, tall, strikingly good-looking dark-haired man. And now that Evie was twenty-one – practically twenty-two – what was left of her mother's considerable financial fortune had passed to her in a trust fund.

That was how it was, Big Joe owned the DuMaret house and properties, but everything else had gone to Evie. Yet even while the monetary riches technically belonged to his daughter, Big Joe had seen to it that it was he himself who kept a tight grip on the proverbial purse strings. He had accomplished this by ensuring that Evie was rarely out of his sight, or at the very least, she was never far from people who were in his employ or under his control. Evie could do nothing without fearing that her daddy was somehow watching her.

It had been like that throughout her sheltered and privileged life, until the shadow of Big Joe Donovan was inextricably bound to her timid conscience. Big Joe had done his job well. Though now of legal age, Evie was ill equipped to have so much as a thought of her own, let alone manage her substantial fortune. So it was up to Big Joe to take care of the money.

In fact, the mere thought of money made Evie's palms sweat. All she knew of money was her father's reputation for accruing it. She knew that her father was equally revered and despised because he knew about money; he could take a little of it and turn it into a lot more. His fortunes were fostered, however, by extended harangues that went on among hostile men behind closed doors.

Evie had no involvement in the making or sustaining of her fortune. And she was in no great hurry to be engaged in tedious, bad-tempered meetings with pasty-faced old bankers. More and more she longed to remain anonymous altogether and far from inquisitive crowds. It was true that in her childhood and well into her teens she had dreamed of love as most girls do. True love, perfect love, the man of mysterious origins who would whisk into her life, take command of her, be severe with her in some vague way and then marry her and rescue her; elevating her existence to something more sublime. Sex had nothing to do with it in those days. Evie knew less of sex than she knew of money.

But what she soon learned of real men quickly snuffed out any idealistic flickering she'd felt about love. More often than not, her over-protective father would be proven right. Men were only after one thing – Evie's fortune. After she'd returned from boarding school, on those rare nights when she would actually have a date, it would never take long for the subject of romance to turn to the fiduciary. What was Evie planning to do with all that money when she came into her trust fund? Every date ended with her feeling disinterested and numb. She'd grown into a pretty young woman while she'd been up north, but it hadn't seemed to matter a bit. The men made no suggestive remarks, no one attempted to seduce her in a dark corner, and in those days they might have found her willing to be seduced.

Now that it had finally come to pass, though – the event the whole town seemed to have been waiting for – now that Evie's trust fund had finally become hers, Evie had less interest than ever in dating. She looked on it more as a social chore. The men who came to call on her (with her father's pre-approval) were spiritually shabby and physically mediocre regardless of their expensive educations or the cut of their hand-tailored suits. Big Joe Donovan had little to fear when it came to the state of his daughter's chastity, her purity and sexual innocence. He knew Evie would never surrender so much as a kiss to any of those dull-witted Lotharios. It wasn't in her to feel lust anymore.

At least not until now. A carnal aching for her spiritual equal fueled these sudden flights into the night alone. A more sophisticated person would have recognized it for what it was, lust, plain and simple. But to Evie it felt like something more precious, a thing she couldn't put words to.

There had never been such a stirring in her before.

And now her daddy had gone and spoiled it as he'd managed to do with everything else that had come along and secretly thrilled her. He had a knack for invading her private world no matter how tightly bottled up she tried to keep it.

Even now under the splendor of the night sky, hidden beneath the majesty of the dark, swooping branches of the ancient oak trees, Evie couldn't ignore her father's presence. Yet he was nowhere near her, he was back at the house, holed up in the master bedroom, a grand suite of rooms that was always off limits to Evie. And whether his lights were on or off, she knew her father's ears were straining for the slightest sound – the screen door inching open or the lightest footstep on the creaking old stairs – to let him know she had come to her senses, that she'd come back home and gone straight to bed.

Bed, her pathetic bed, the place where more often than not she lay awake until all hours and stared blankly at the walls. It was that god-awful bed, the hulking antique mahogany four-poster draped in mosquito netting, as if the old house had never been rewired for central air conditioning. It was that claustrophobic piece of ancient furniture that had sent her out in search of something less constraining, a place where her thoughts could soar. She'd found that place amidst the trees, beneath a canopy of living things that had witnessed the triumphs of her grandparents and her great-grandparents and perhaps the agony of a thousand slaves and anyone else who had come before her.

The thoughts Evie found herself entertaining in this unrestrictive space intrigued her profoundly. The unlikelihood of her existence, for one thing, that especially intrigued her. Why had she been born? Was it to achieve some sort of greatness? If not, then why had her mother died so suddenly after giving birth to her? From this angle, it almost looked as if the sole purpose of Evie's mother's life had been to give birth to a baby and die.

A baby, she thought, me, I was that baby. I was meant to be conceived.

For a moment, she was reminded of the unthinkable. There was clearly at least one other thing her mother had done in her brief life – she had gotten fucked by Evie's daddy. Then her mother had given birth to a baby and died.

Her thoughts flitted away from that idea because it made her too uncomfortable. The thought of her father fucking anyone at all confused her. What was that, anyway, fucking? What did that mean when you really thought about it? Sex was a quagmire, a bog of unsettling urges, searing thoughts that sprang out of nowhere like a flash fire, then sank into feelings of suffocation and oppression. She didn't understand sex at all. What little she knew of it she had gleaned from watching a porno movie on cable TV once. She'd stumbled upon it accidentally, very late one fateful, eye-popping night. But the television was in her father's study, just off his master suite. It was not where she wanted to be learning about sex, and not the baby-making stuff they'd taught her about at school either, but the real thing, the goods, the dirty urges that made normal people fly out of the house at all hours and ravenously begin dating.

Immediately, Evie had seen the appeal of sex. She wasn't that pathetic, she understood it. She saw the appeal of everything, fellatio, cunnilingus, and intercourse in all its many provocative positions. While every detail of the sordid acts was spread out before her eyes in living color on a forty-two inch screen, she was hooked. Sex was lewd and lascivious, that's what it was, but the lurid images drew her like a magnet into irresistible territory for a good forty-five minutes. She wanted to take off her clothes right there in front of the TV set and figure herself out. Why did she have to be a virgin? How could she rectify that? It was then that she'd finally come to her senses, however. Her father frequently stayed out late, but he never stayed out all night and Evie wanted to be far from his study whenever he did manage to make it home.

So she'd gone back to her own room. She'd kept her clothes on, kept her virginity, and forced herself to turn off the TV, but the ideas it had filled her with that night were unbearable. The inescapable urgency to experience sex swelled up inside her, and like a sultry ooze it filled her dark room with lust, oppressively thick and peculiarly impenetrable. She'd never been so horny in all her life.

Evie had thought then about the lackluster men she sometimes dated, but she'd quickly realized none of them would ever do. And she wondered now what it was even for this lust, this insatiable urge to sin. Why bother when real men were so dull?

A night bird called out over her head. It sang out jubilantly and startled her by how close it was. And somewhere hidden in the distance came the equally joyful reply of its mate, a rustling of wings, and then the night was quiet again.

How long had she been standing there?

Evie realized that she'd managed to break her father's spell; she wasn't worrying about him father anymore or what he might be expecting of her.

She wandered deeper into the tangle of trees, mindful to keep her exposed legs clear of the places where she knew there would likely be poison oak and probably poison sumac, too. She reached a small clearing where an enormous cold black rock jutted up from the bowels of the earth, and the tree branches overhead parted to reveal an inspiring patch of sky.

Evie leaned against the rock, her bare legs pressing against the cold hard slab of it, finding it refreshing against her warm skin in the humid night air. She wanted to pull her shorts down then, so she did.

She was practically naked out there in the darkness. But who was there to come along and spy on her? A person would have to know those trees by heart to even find her, so she didn't care. Only a few nights ago she'd actually done it, stripped right out of her clothes and touched herself right there against that very rock. She had spread her legs wide and touched herself in the moonlight. She had touched herself until she came. But tonight there was no moon and the stars seemed unusually far away. Her heart grew heavy and she didn't understand why.

She lowered her panties down her thighs and made a half-hearted attempt to excite herself, her fingers working between her legs.

It was all the useless, empty days, she realized. Everyone was waiting for her to get married turn all her money over to someone else. That's all it was about.

Now she wasn't excited at all. She felt more disgusted than anything else. She pulled her panties back up around her hips and then pulled on her shorts. She thought again about her mother, and suddenly it seemed more than sufficient to live long enough to have a baby and then die. Pass that money down the line to the next of kin and forget about it. Her poor mother had probably been bored to death with it all and that's why she had died, from the boredom.

But what did that mean if it was true, if her mother hadn't wanted to live? Did it mean her mother hadn't really loved her daddy? Did it mean there hadn't been some grand passion pulling them into matrimony to create her? That it had all been about money?

She panicked. That couldn't be true. There was no truth in it whatsoever! There was more to her fine heritage than simply money. And yet... no, this wouldn't do. These thoughts were taking her nowhere. She'd come out here to feel excited by life and now all she could feel was despair.

Evie left the rock and worked her way back through the tangle of trees the way she'd come, only now she felt lost as she headed for the sameness of home.

Chapter Two

The following morning, Vera, the housekeeper, woke Evie at the crack of dawn. "I'm sorry to get you up so early, honey," she apologized softly, pulling aside the mosquito netting, "but your daddy wanted me to check on you before he left for work."

Evie was curled down deep in her blankets; the air conditioning was working overtime. "Check on me?" she inquired sleepily. "What's that supposed to mean? To make sure I'm all right in the head, or to make sure I'm not laying here with some man?"

"It's nothing so sinister, honey," Vera assured her. "He just wants me to make sure you're all right. He's worried about you. I am, too. You've been acting awful queer lately."

"You don't mean that the way it sounds, do you? I may not go out with many men, Vera, but I've never gone out with girls."

Vera was momentarily taken aback, but then she smiled. "You be careful, Evie. Your mama's sense of humor is starting to show."

For as long as Evie could remember, Vera had always acted as if it were something to guard against, Evie exhibiting any behavior traits reminiscent of her late mother's.

"Vera," Evie ventured, "did my daddy love my mother? I mean, were they in love like lovers? Did they have a torrid passion or did they marry for more practical reasons like money?"

Vera was stopped short by Evie's impertinence. "What kind of a question is that, young lady, and why this sudden interest in things long gone? It's not good to dwell on it."

"Well, what kind of an answer is that?" Evie countered. "That's no kind of answer at all. It's like you're admitting that there was no passion between them. Is that why I'm never allowed to behave like my mother, because my daddy found everything about her so distasteful, except maybe her inheritance?"

"Evie Donovan!" Vera gasped. "Who's putting these horrible ideas into your head? Your mama loved your daddy more than life itself, and vice versa. That is a well known fact."

"That's true enough, it seems to be a fact that's very well known." But something about it struck a note of discord in Evie and always had. Since time immemorial, it seemed as if everyone spoke of the passing of Clarice DuMaret Donovan as the day time itself had stopped, or the calendar had run out of pages forever, or the day Big Joe Donovan's heart had been shattered, destroying him for good, making it so that he couldn't so much as look at another woman as long as he lived. "Hogwash," she muttered.

"Evie, honey, what is it?" Vera sat down tentatively on the edge of the bed.

"Nothing, Vera, it's nothing that I want to talk about because no one around here gives me a straight answer, anyway."

The housekeeper was clearly troubled. "Haven't you always been able to come to me, honey? Haven't I always been there for you when you've had something on your mind?"

Of course, Evie thought to herself, you've been just like a mother to me. Only you're not my mother and you never will be.

"Why don't you tell me what's going on with you, Evie?"

"You mean where am I slipping off to at night? Can't I have any privacy around here? I told my daddy last night, I'm over twenty-one, Vera. I don't have to tell you everything. I'm tired of this."

"Tired of what?"

"This life, living like this under a microscope all the time… I'm tired of life."

The housekeeper looked alarmed, as if maybe Evie were talking about suicide. Then Evie alarmed her even more. "Who were the Donovans, Vera?"

"What?"

"The Donovans, my father's family, who were they and how come nobody ever talks about them? Where did they go? It seems like the whole town knows everything about the DuMarets. What happened to the Donovan side of the family? Aren't there even any pictures?"

Vera stood up suddenly. "Evie, it's getting late. Your daddy's going to leave for work soon and I still have to serve him his breakfast." She left the room abruptly, slamming the door closed behind her.

It was Evie's turn to be taken aback. "Was it something I said?" she called half-heartedly to no one.

***

"It's time for Evie to have a life of her own, Mr. Donovan,"

Vera said more calmly as she began clearing away the breakfast dishes. "That's all it is. You can't keep her little forever, you know that, she's more than old enough to be on her own and living her own life, starting a family, even. She's restless cooped up out here."

Big Joe finished what was left of his breakfast in two quick gulps. He got up from the table and tossed his crumpled napkin down onto his empty plate. "Did you find out where she's been going off to at night?" he asked as if he hadn't heard a word Vera had said.

"No," Vera answered, "I didn't."

"Maybe it's time to find her a husband," he relented. "Maybe I need to start looking into that. Someone who's good with money, who'll give her a nice home, who'll keep her from roaming around at night and maybe getting herself into trouble, if it isn't too late. You don't think she could be getting herself into trouble, do you? This has all the earmarks of a boy, if you ask me."

Vera looked helpless. She didn't have a clue.

Big Joe went out into the foyer and prepared to leave for work.

Vera followed close on his heels. "She's been asking about her mother again," she said quietly.

"Really?"

"Questions about you and Clarice."

"What kind of questions?"

"Whether or not you were in love with her. And now she wants to know about the Donovans, too."

Big Joe glanced up the winding staircase in the direction of his daughter's room. "Maybe I'd better have a little talk with her right now," he said, "before this goes any further." And then he added, thinking aloud on his way up the stairs, "I'm going to have Cal Harper come home with me for supper one night this week. He'd make a good match for Evie. His family's got nothing but money and he's just about her age."

Big Joe stopped in at Evie's room. Her bedroom door was slightly ajar, but he tapped on it anyway to be polite, trying to make up for how he'd slammed the front door in her face the night before. It was a gesture of apology – a rarity, coming from Big Joe – but it was wasted on Evie. She wasn't in her room. "Evie?" he called out quietly, but there was no answer. Then he glanced surreptitiously around her room. He wasn't sure what he was looking for, really, but he felt relieved just the same. Everything seemed to be in place. It was just her head that was getting cluttered up inside and he'd take care of that soon enough.

On his way back down the hall, he stopped in his own room, and to his complete surprise, found Evie.

The surprise was unquestionably mutual. "Hey daddy!" she exclaimed, nearly jumping out of her skin. "I thought you'd gone to work."

She was still in her nightgown, a short, flowery affair, and her light brown hair was still a tousled mess from another restless night of sleep. She wasn't even wearing her slippers, as if she'd been in that much of a hurry to start nosing around his room. Standing awkwardly next to his unmade bed, she looked guilty as hell.

"Evie, what are you doing in here?"

"Nothing, daddy."

"You know what?" he snapped, "I'm getting damn tired of hearing that answer. You're not supposed to be in here, now what the hell are you doing?"

Her palms were beginning to sweat and her heart was racing. Her father's night table drawer was standing open and the contents were strewn on the bed. She wondered how long it would be before he noticed.

Not long.

"What are you doing?" he shouted, approaching her as he saw his private life, his mementoes, his secrets, scattered all over the bed. He scanned the items quickly. There were a few old keys (he couldn't remember where they'd come from) some ancient snapshots with tattered edges (nothing salacious or incriminating there, thank God) some old bank receipts and scraps of paper (notes to himself, harmless). Regrettably, what seemed to be intriguing his daughter most were the handful of old postcards, none written on, from that tacky motel lounge just outside of town where the men from Baton Rouge would stay before Clarice went crazy, before the wild days came to a grinding halt. He wouldn't have to explain a bunch of blank postcards, would he? His heart lurched a bit when he recognized the small white bible that had belonged to Clarice, but there was no harm in that coming to light. And then he saw it, the old letter lying in a crumpled heap on his bed.

Big Joe's instincts told him to grab it, to shield his daughter before it was too late, but he didn't want to make any sudden moves toward it. He knew a move like that would only bring his daughter back again when his back was turned, and then she would be in hot pursuit of the letter until she found it. Evie was too curious. In too many ways, she was exactly like Clarice.

Big Joe's anger was acute, but he tried to be patient. He couldn't let this blow out of proportion. "Have you found what you're looking for?"

"I wasn't looking for anything!"

"Evie," he said, "look at yourself! How can you stand there and lie to me, right to my face? You were going through my things. What were you looking for?"

He didn't wait for her answer, he knew what she was looking for – proof; proof of a love between himself and Clarice. He picked up the small white bible. "Here," he said, thinking fast and giving it to her, "why don't you have this? It was your mother's. I'd always meant to give it to you anyway." Then he scooped up the rest of the contents from the bed and tossed them quickly back in the drawer.

But not the letter, the letter he slipped into his pocket while Evie was distracted by the unexpected gift of her late mother's bible. Then he rifled through the contents of another drawer until he found a book of matches he had been saving. "Here," he said, giving that to her, too.

"What's this?" she asked, taking it suspiciously.

"A memento," he told her.

The matchbook cover had a lurid drawing on it of a woman. She was topless and wore high heels. Her large breasts were very pointy and her scantily clad ass was tiny and round. The sexy figure was cuddling up to a giant martini glass. The name of the establishment was written across the top of the book of matches, The Hi Life Motel and beneath it was the address, Alliance off Highway 61.

"It's not there anymore," he said.

"But what's it a memento of?" she asked, bewildered. Why would her father be handing her something as racy as this?

"It's where your mother and I spent our honeymoon."

"Your honeymoon?"

"We were in a hurry."

"In a hurry? What does that mean?"

"I'll explain it to you some other time, Evie, I need to get to work, I'm late. Now get your butt out of here and don't let me catch you doing this again." He took here by the arm, less roughly than he'd done the night before, but just as emphatically, and escorted her out of his room. "And listen," he said, pulling the door closed, "I'm bringing someone to supper later this week, Cal Harper. You be nice to him, Evie."

She understood what that meant. She knew that tone of voice. Her daddy was fixing her up with a man, another useless, boring man. She glared at her father, and her father glared right back at her.

"You need to get out more," he said. "That's final."

***

Big Joe's driver had been waiting patiently all this time, leaning lazily against the shining black Lincoln as the early morning sun crept up steadily, burning a wide path of sunshine through the heavy, hazy sky. When Big Joe finally came out onto the porch, Thomas, beginning to sweat in his black uniform from the already thick humidity, jumped to attention and opened the car door.

"I need to go straight to my meeting, Thomas. I don't have time to stop in at the office now." The meeting was all the way in New Orleans, a good hour-and-a-half drive, in one of Big Joe's sparkling glass high-rise towers just west of the French Quarter. He was preparing to hire a new recruit, someone who was purported to be nothing less than impeccably discreet and reliable, fresh blood, a veritable right hand man, someone to take the place of Bert Hannon, who until recently had been Big Joe's most trusted associate. But Bert was too riddled with ulcers and anxiety these days to be of much use to the business. Friendships were one thing, but when it came to business, Big Joe wanted only assets, not liabilities, and what good was Bert now if he'd lost his nerve? So Big Joe had retired him.

At age fifty-two, Bert hadn't gone willingly. Where else was he likely to be employed, he'd argued, when he'd spent his whole damn life being nothing but a whitewashed procurer for Big Joe Donovan's insatiable greed? "I know where all the bodies are buried," Bert had warned him, wincing in pain, looking bleak and worn as he popped another antacid, the petty threats coming out of his mouth making him seem even more pathetic. It had gotten ugly, which was a damn shame. Big Joe hated to see a life long friend reduced to impotent bitterness.

He took a bottle of cold water from the car's mini bar and gave some thought now to Evie. She was usually so docile and easily controlled. She was becoming a bit of a liability herself, in a way. Maybe the poor little fool just needed to get laid. Hopefully he could marry her off before too much damage was done in that department. Then he remembered the letter in his pocket. He would have to find a safer place for it. He absently fingered the aging envelope and thought of the Hi Life Motel. It had been a run down disreputable place, practically condemned even back then. Talk about needing to get laid, he remembered. Talk about too much damage being done. Why hadn't he helped her? Why hadn't he seen what he was doing?

Then one by one his failures came back to him in unerring detail, the memories surging in on him like waves. He stared distractedly out the darkened window of the Lincoln, helpless to stop the onslaught of his past, and for the remainder of the drive to the city, Big Joe buried Clarice all over again.

Chapter Three

Evie set her mother's bible aside and stared again at the book of matches in her hand. "The Hi Life motel," she said softly. "Alliance off Highway 61... that would have been clear into New Orleans," she figured. She began to see her parents in a whole new light.

They couldn't wait to get laid, she realized. That's what the rush had been about, sex, passion, lust, all those things that she herself could understand now. That's what cheap motels were for. Still, they would have needed it to be legal. They would have needed to get married first, so it became 'their honey-moon'. She knew her father could be a ruthless man, but he wouldn't have done anything less than honorable by her mother. Clarice had had a sterling reputation. The whole town had always said so. But now Evie saw that her mother had probably been just a little bit human, too.

A pretty white bible and a book of matches from a cheap motel... what an interesting person Clarice DuMaret was turning out to be.

The day was already in full swing before Evie decided to get dressed. As she slid into her shorts and pulled on a cotton shirt, she realized she felt envious of her parents. They'd had a real love, passion even, and here she was going to have to sit through yet another disastrous dinner with another tedious man no closer to love than she'd been before. It was enough to make her want to cry, but she was tired of tears. They never helped anything and only made her feel more pathetic.

Cal Harper. On her way downstairs, she searched her brain for any recollections she might have of Cal Harper, of having ever crossed his path, but her mind came up blank. He was probably from the city, she decided, rich as hell with a heart as empty of life as an abandoned graveyard. But he'd be polite. His hands would be like ice, but his manners would be impeccable. Evie already knew that from experience. These men were all so civilized, but their collective lack of fire and imagination filled her with contempt.

She went out onto the veranda and plunked her weary self down on the porch swing.

Another day, another hot, humid, oppressive day with nowhere to go and nothing to do except wait for the torture to be over.

***

The express elevator shot up to the twenty-ninth floor in one smooth, nearly undetectable motion. The doors opened silently onto an outer office so opulent, it was hard to believe it was merely the entryway to something even grander. The sophisticated décor spoke in hushed tones of elegant modernism. Highly polished maple walls, recessed lighting, and frosted glass created soothing geometric patterns that were a far cry from the colorful, cloying decay of the cramped French Quarter not far below.

When Lucas Cain stepped out of the elevator, Susie, the receptionist, did a double take. He was almost too good-looking, this man. Did they really make men like him? It instantly set her nerves on edge. Though calm and collected, something about him smoldered, and men like that didn't usually have appointments at Donovan & Company. Susie had seen plenty of dusty laborers in Levi's and hard hats, and brittle uptight bankers who were never less than a century old. There were the occasional Ivy Leaguers from up north, young men, mostly who smiled a lot but clearly held themselves above everybody, and they always managed to look as if they'd bathed in milk. But never had a man like this made it to the twenty-ninth floor.

He sure knows how to make an entrance, she thought. That elevator had never spit out anything as handsome as him. "May I help you?" she asked sweetly.

"I'm Lucas Cain," he said with intimidating self-possession. "I have a nine o'clock. with Mr. Donovan."

She checked her computer for the day's appointments. She knew full well that someone named Lucas Cain had a nine o'clock, it was the only reason Big Joe Donovan had stepped foot into the building at all, but she wanted to buy herself some time. From the corner of her eye she studied him, his tall, dark and handsome persona that simply didn't seem real and his impeccably tailored clothes. He was straight out of a fantasy of what men were supposed to look like. He had to be at least six-foot-two, black hair, black eyes, slim but solid. Everything about him seemed rock hard and, in spite of herself, the thought of how rock hard he was made her a little wet. He was a perfect specimen, and she hoped she would be seeing more of him. He made the normally cool, detached atmosphere of the office seem suddenly on fire. "Yes," she said at last, "here you are, nine o'clock. Why don't you have a seat and I'll see if Mr. Donovan's ready for you? He's only just arrived."

Lucas didn't move. He stood in front of her desk and openly studied her, his coal-black eyes taking in every inch of her hair, and she wondered uneasily if what was underneath her sweater was measuring up to his approval.

"Please," she managed to say, "have a seat. It could be a few minutes."

"I'm fine," he told her with a warm smile full of genuine charm and masculine ease. His voice caressed her ears with an undertone of solicitation. "I don't mind standing," he said. "My legs haven't failed me yet."

"All right," she relented, but it felt rude to resume her work with him standing so close to her, looking down at her, doing nothing but watching her. She should make conversation, but her mind drew a blank. She wanted to give him her phone number, ask him to lunch, take him to bed and run her manicured fingers through his thick black hair, but none of those things were even remotely appropriate, so instead she just smiled politely for several awkward moments.

"You can bring Mr. Cain in now, Susie." Miss Morrow finally buzzed her.

Obediently, Susie rose and had Lucas Cain follow her down the endless marble hall to Miss Morrow's office, and she prayed the entire way that those hard hours at the gym were now working their mighty miracles on her pert and very available rear end. She hoped Lucas Cain was mesmerized by what she knew he was staring at.

"Miss Morrow, this is Mr. Cain," Susie announced, leading Lucas into Miss Morrow's sterile and inhospitable office of stainless steel and beveled glass. She took catty pleasure in watching Miss Morrow take one look at Lucas Cain, shoot out of her chair like a rocket, and then try in vain to drop ten years and twenty pounds in the short time it took her to come around to the front of her enormous desk and shake Lucas Cain's hand.

"I'm Miss Morrow," she practically gushed, "Mr. Donovan's personal secretary. Let me take you in to him. He's very eager to make your acquaintance. You've come so highly recommended… that'll be all, Susie. You can go now."

Susie left reluctantly as Miss Morrow led Lucas through the connecting vestibule, and then into Big Joe Donovan's private office.

"Mr. Donovan," Miss Morrow announced, managing to keep her cool, "this is Mr. Cain."

Big Joe sat behind his impressive desk smoking a cigarette. A cup of coffee sat in front of him, untouched. His dark, brooding eyes seemed lost in thought. He glanced up as Lucas Cain came in, but he didn't ask him to sit down. He didn't say hello. He just stared at him hard, hostility creeping into the cold stone of his face. Finally, he spoke. "Thank you, Miss Morrow," he said. "That'll be all."

Big Joe's office was a testament to power. Everything had been designed to keep a visitor ill at ease. The well-appointed space was long, with Big Joe's desk set at the far end of it. This required a visitor to walk, unprotected and vulnerable, for a good stretch under Big Joe's calculated gaze. Seating was strategic, too. The chairs were exquisitely upholstered, but designed to be just low enough to put the person sitting in one of them at an uncomfortable disadvantage to Big Joe's overpowering desk. And the sightline was such that the visitor was compelled to constantly look up in a posture of worship or subservience.

I've seen this one before, Big Joe thought, but where?

Lucas was unflappable. He stood just inside Big Joe's office, and let him stare. He'd wait until he was invited to sit down or to speak. He was in no hurry. He'd come this far, he had nothing he needed to prove.

"Lucas Cain." Big Joe pronounced the name with quiet purpose, stubbing out his cigarette. "Where do I know you from, Cain? I do know you, don't I?"

"I'm impressed," Lucas replied casually, "I was much younger then."

"Just spill it. I don't need to be entertained."

"It was in the French Quarter," Lucas told him, "many years ago."

Big Joe did not look pleased. "Where exactly in the French Quarter?"

"Miss Willie's old place on Royal Street, by Esplanade Avenue. I was a lot younger, just a kid really, but then you were younger, too."

Big Joe's voice was void of any emotion. "Miss Willie's..." he said, turning the memories over in his mind. A high-class house of ill repute, it had been one of Clarice's favorite haunts. Who could know about Miss Willie's? This was nothing but bad news. He had to stay on his toes. "And what would a boy be doing in a place like that?"

"Fetching," Lucas answered.

"Fetching," Big Joe echoed skeptically.

"Yes, fetching, running after whatever the customers needed

in exchange for tips, loose change, that sort of thing. When I was a kid, I was dirt poor."

Lucas now had every ounce of Big Joe's attention. The mere sound of the words 'dirt poor' unnerved Big Joe.

"One night you came in late," Lucas went on, "with your wife. A very pretty young thing, dressed to the nines. She'd taken ill, and you had me fetch her something from over on Pirate's Alley, behind that little corner bar, there was a man waiting for me. He handed me a tiny paper packet. You gave me a twenty-dollar bill for running that errand. Until then, I'd never held a twenty-dollar bill in my life. I was fourteen years old."

Big Joe's stone face slackened. "Luke," he said. "I'll be a son of a bitch!"

"I know," Lucas said as if he understood the irony of that remark.

"I'm a little surprised you're even alive. Talk about poor. Jesus, you were one wretched kid, and now look at you."

Lucas Cain's pride was inching up his throat, but he kept it in check. "I owe it all to you, Donovan. You gave me some good advice once, and I took it to heart."

"I did?"

"Yes, you told me it was a crime against nature to be poor, and that staying poor was a choice, not a life sentence."

Big Joe was caught off guard again, but he didn't show it. This man is aiming too close to home, he thought. "I said that?" he asked suspiciously.

"You did."

Big Joe stood up and motioned to a chair. "Why don't you sit down, Cain, and tell me why you're here."

Lucas refused to sit. "You know why I'm here. I've come about a job."

Noticing the gold watch Lucas wore and the diamond pinky ring on his finger, Big Joe said, "You don't strike me as a man who needs a job."

"Well, I don't think you're really offering a job, are you, Donovan? It's more like a commitment to a career."

"That it is," Big Joe conceded.

"I have the experience needed for that type of career."

"You're sure of that?"

"I am," he said. "I know my way around. I worked my way up the hard way, but I did it the right way. I have a real estate license and I'm a licensed contractor. I also have a license to shoot firearms. I keep everything legal. As I'm sure you've already discovered, my record is clean, no felonies. Now, what would you say to getting out of this overbearing office for a while and going to more neutral territory so we can really discuss this?"

"Don't tell me. You know a little place on Royal Street."

***

Lucas signaled the waitress for two coffees. The café was dingy and dark even though the morning was sunny, and like most of the small establishments in the Quarter, it was not air-conditioned. It opened right onto the street. On the ceiling, two ancient fans whirred through the air. It was thick, humid air, but at least it moved.

Big Joe felt conspicuous. He wondered why he had agreed to this. It was because of Evie stirring up all those memories of Clarice. "I haven't been down in the Quarter in years," he said.

"I know."

"And how do you know that?"

Lucas shrugged. "Word gets around. If you'd come back to

the Quarter, I would have heard about it. Let's face it, certain people remember you, and I'm not just talking about Royal Street."

The waitress set the coffees on the table and walked away.

"I know you stayed a player, Donovan. After your wife died, you bought up half this town. It's just that Bert Hannon showed up at meetings in lieu of you. He suffered the foul smells of the Quarter so you didn't have to. I can only assume the French Quarter smells particularly foul to a man like you, how couldn't it?"

"Meaning?"

"Meaning you spent your halcyon days here, Donovan. I know that, I remember, I saw you spending them. You and your wife had the world on a string in those days. You know, I idolized you. I didn't want to be poor, who in their right mind does? You and your wife made it seem so... I don't know, preferable to be rich. I couldn't help but notice that after she died you never came back. I can only assume the memories around here were too much for you, so you sent Bert Hannon instead."

"Don't assume anything, Cain." For once, Big Joe was uncertain how to play his hand. He'd had Cain's background thoroughly checked. In a way, he couldn't risk not hiring him. Cain was a professional in all the right ways, as though he'd come readymade for Donovan & Company. But the background check hadn't turned up that Cain had known him before, that he remembered Clarice. How could it? A background check reveals the facts, not the stuff inside a man's head. "What do you know of Solisville?" he asked.

"Not much," Lucas admitted, unbuttoning his suit jacket and leaning back in his chair. All eyes in the dark café were on him, at least the female eyes, and the waitress's especially. Lucas was used to it. He could feel the attention he was getting though he made a point never to acknowledge it. That could only lead to problems. Eye contact led to unwelcome overtures, solicitous conversations and sex was a minefield, too distracting. It altered a man's judgment and could become a man's downfall. Lucas had seen it happen before. "I know that at one time," he went on, "your wife's family practically owned Solisville, but you're the man in control now. It's a small town, but you own just about everything, including a newspaper, The Evening Call, and a local television station. You throw lavish parties twice a year and everyone who's anyone in Solisville is expected to attend. The town is flat, affluent, and usually very green. Your house," Lucas paused before continuing, "your house was expensively renovated after your wife passed away. It's quite impressive, and it was once the property of the DuMarets."

"You've seen my house then?"

"Only the outside of it. It's not as if your address is a secret, Donovan."

Big Joe couldn't help but feel impressed. This man was nothing if not prepared. But there was also something a little off-putting about him, maybe because he reminded Big Joe too much of himself. He stubbed out a half-smoked cigarette, and then gulped down the rest of his coffee. He pushed back his chair and stood up to go. "I have an office there in Solisville, as I'm sure you know. It's where I spend most of my time. I don't come into New Orleans that often. And as you also know, I usually stay clear of the Quarter altogether. I would expect you to spend a lot of your time in Solisville, too. Tell me something," he asked in all honesty, "do you have a life of your own, Cain?"

"No," Lucas assured him. "How could I? Like you, my work is my life."

"That's where you're wrong. I have a personal life, Cain. I have a daughter. I had a wife. I pity you," he added. "But then I pity a lot of people, it's nothing unusual. Come out to my place tonight and we'll continue this."

"I'll be there with bells on, Donovan."

"I wouldn't be a bit surprised."

Chapter Four

When Big Joe stepped out into the sunlight, Thomas pulled the black Lincoln up to the curb in front of the café. Big Joe didn't wait for Thomas to get out and open the door for him; he opened it himself and got inside. The car was dark and cool. He leaned back in the luxury of the leather seat and stared ahead of him blankly. He couldn't help but feel the dice were loaded. Lucas Cain knew all the right things, but he knew too much about Clarice. That could become a problem. But at the first hint of blackmail, Big Joe would pick up the phone, plain and simple. He would do it without blinking. There was Evie to think of. He owed Clarice that much.

"Where to, sir?" Thomas asked.

Big Joe realized they were still sitting in the middle of Royal Street.

"Let's get out of here," he said. "I've got work to do."

***

Lucas walked the few blocks to where he had parked his car over on Clinton Place. He drove an unassuming black two-door convertible, but he almost always kept the top up. He got in the car and headed for home. The first order of business would be to ditch the suit and tie. He was decidedly not the suit and tie type unless it was absolutely required.

When he reached his street it was obvious that anyone with half a brain was working a sensible day job. His street was deserted and he liked it that way. His world was nobody's business. He pulled his car up the narrow driveway and got out.

His was a house common to the Lower Garden District, a two-story wooden structure, narrow and long, with the typical covered gallery across the front that helped shield the house from the relentless New Orleans heat. The gallery, top and bottom, was supported by Greek columns and decorated with the ubiquitous cast iron detailing. The house itself was hidden behind a wildly overgrown garden of thriving banana trees and cashmere bouquet, but behind the tangle of greenery one could see that it was painted off-white, and that the floor-to-ceiling shutters that covered the front windows upstairs and down were an unassuming dull blue. And like every other house in New Orleans, its paint was peeling from the never-ending rain and humidity.

Lucas lived alone. He was practically undressed before he reached the bedroom upstairs. He hung his suit meticulously in his closet, next to the other suits he hated to wear, all of them pressed and organized by color.

In nothing but his white cotton briefs and a thin gold chain around his neck, he collapsed across the bed. The room was sweltering. The shutters were closed against the sun and the overhead fan whirled at top speed. He began to sweat. He made a mental note to change the sheets before he got back into bed that night. He hated nothing less than perfectly clean sheets. He was of the opinion that only poor people slept on dirty sheets, as he had done as a boy. Out of habit, he examined his fingernails to ensure that they, too, were clean. Finally, he thought. I've been invited inside, on my own merits.

The old DuMaret mansion up the river road that he'd fanta-sized about since he was a poor boy in the Vieux Carré... it was as if the final mystery were being unveiled. He had been invited inside. Next, he told himself, he would probably be invited for dinner. The day would come when he would be in and out of that legendary house as if he'd been doing it, not just dreaming about it, all his life. He would come to know Solisville like the back of his hand.

For Lucas Cain, this was success, being on equal footing with the great man himself, with Big Joe Donovan, who had been his salvation as a boy. The man who'd guided Lucas out of the prison of poverty, even though he didn't seem to remember he'd done it. But wasn't that usually the case? A person could have a profound influence on a youngster and never have a clue it was happening. For Lucas, Big Joe Donovan had been living proof that anyone could achieve the improbable. He could go from utter poverty to a seat at the head of the DuMaret's lavish table. All a man needed was patience, like Donovan had had in going after Clarice, patience and a few good schemes. It had paid off for Donovan in spades and now Lucas was going to be in that same impressive company of people who had gone from rags to riches.

His cock was getting hard, bulging in his briefs. It was aching for attention. Lucas always got a hard-on when his ego was stroked, as if the two were connected. Success gave him a killer erection. He yanked down his briefs and gave into it. He worked his cock vigorously in his fist, his muscles tightening, his rock-hard body acutely responsive. It wasn't long before he was drenched in sweat.

He summoned his dream girl to the forefront of his imagination. She was a dark-haired beauty, naked and compliant. He fucked her in his head, and he fucked her hard, with extreme vigor, his mind savoring every lewd position his imagination could put her in.

His fantasy girl was his best-kept secret. Her insatiable appetite for sex had helped him through years of loneliness. She was the woman who was always eager to please him, to spread her legs for him without complaining. And what no one would have ever guessed, the secret he treasured most, was that his dream girl was Donovan's late wife, Clarice, or at least how Lucas remembered her, had embellished her, over the years. Clarice had been the first beautiful woman Lucas had ever seen naked. The vision had been fleeting, but it had stayed with him, become an obsession early on, until he never jerked off without thinking of Clarice. He'd been only fourteen when it had happened, and it had happened by accident; he'd seen Clarice naked by mistake. But he'd seen her, he'd seen everything, in fact, and he'd been overwhelmed by it, by how erotic she had looked. This had been back in the days at Miss Willie's.

That night, Big Joe had been locked in some downstairs room with the gamblers, those men from Baton Rouge. Clarice was upstairs, doing what she called 'entertaining' in a room where the smell of opium was strong. She'd sent for him that night; she'd wanted Lucas to come to her room. She'd asked for another bottle of champagne and Lucas had brought it to her. He knew enough to knock before entering, but it hadn't made a difference. Clarice was naked when he went in. It had seemed to Lucas that she didn't even realize she wasn't wearing any clothes. It was the other man in the room who had told Clarice to put on her kimono, but it was too late, Lucas had gotten an eyeful.

Later that night, alone in that smelly bed Miss Willie provided for him in lieu of a paycheck, Lucas obsessed about Clarice. He explored her body in vivid detail while jerking himself off into a grimy sheet. And now it was simply a habit. When Lucas's cock was hard, when his hand was wrapped around it, up sprang the vision of Clarice, a nimble and very willing partner in his imaginary world.

Chapter 5

In the dining room that evening, Evie sat across the dinner table from her father and tried hard to pay attention to what he was saying, but he was going on again about Cal Harper, his background and his successes as a young businessman in his father's import/export company.

"He's not much older than you, Evie. You've probably got a lot in common."

This was supposed to make the man sound appealing, this fragment of common ground. "I don't care how old he is, daddy," she protested. "I can't imagine we'll have anything to talk about. He'll probably spend the whole evening wanting to talk about money."

"I'm going to help you through this one, Evie. We'll all have supper together, right here, on Thursday night. There'll be things to talk about besides money, you'll see. You're not getting out of this one, so you'd better resign yourself to making a good impression. Don't embarrass me. I've known Cal's father for a long time."

Evie poked at her food with a fork. The plan was only slightly more attractive than the usual escapade – dinner at Solisville's only upscale restaurant, The Tropical Breeze, where every nosey parker in the place would be eyeing Evie and her date. At least this time she would have the luxury of being bored to tears in private.

"And wear something pretty, make an effort."

"Why should I make an effort? It's too depressing. No one could care less about what I'm wearing or what I look like. I'm just a walking bank account."

But it was as if Evie were talking to a wall now. Her father's attention was elsewhere. He'd been moodier than usual the whole evening and Evie couldn't help but feel it was her fault, that this had something to do with what had happened that morning bringing up all those memories of her mother. She regarded her father curiously as he stared into space and tried to picture it, what he had looked like in the old days before she was born, back when he had been in love with her mother, when her mother had been very much alive, the two of them together on their wedding night drawn into some sort of sexual frenzy in the Hi Life Motel. She figured her father had probably been very good-looking then, after all he was still attractive now, his black hair just slightly graying at the temples and a few lines on his face. But he was still broad shouldered and tall, with coal black eyes that could still flash with feeling, especially when he was angry with her. For the first time, it occurred to her that the sixty-year-old man sitting across the dinner table from her had once been a young man of passion, maybe even a man of dreams and ambitions. But could rich men ever really be called ambitious? How could a man have ambitions if he already had plenty of money, if he'd been born rich, like her daddy had? What would there be to be ambitious about?

"Who were the Donovans?" she asked suddenly. "They weren't from Solisville, were they?"

Big Joe didn't answer. He acted like he hadn't even heard her. "Evie, I don't want you getting into any trouble. If there's some boy you've been seeing at night, it has to stop. I know you're twenty-one, and I know you don't like being told what to do anymore, but if a boy can't call on you in broad daylight, if he can't come here and meet me in person and make his intentions known, then he isn't a boy you should be associating with. You're too young to know yet what men can be like, but I do, I know. I know what men are after."

"There isn't any boy, daddy."

"I think you should try to learn how to appreciate young men like Cal Harper, whom you say are only interested in money. They have your best interests at heart. They're not going to bleed you dry of your inheritance. They'll help you turn your fortune into an even bigger one. You'll never have to want for anything."

Except love, she thought.

"I'm not going to live forever, honey," he went on. "I'd like to know that you have a good, solid future ahead of you, that your affairs will be in good hands when I'm gone."

Evie wanted to be excused from the table. Her father was talking right through her again as if all she was made of were money, as if who she really was didn't matter at all. She didn't figure into the equation of any marriage, only her inheritance did. "I'm tired," she said. "I want to go to my room now."

Big Joe was exasperated. There was no getting through to her.

"Fine, Evie," he said, his patience gone. "Go to your room, but explain to me one thing. Why is it that you can't stay in your room? Where is it you're going at night? Just tell me!"

"Nowhere, daddy!" she replied, just as exasperated. "I already told you, there isn't any boy. I'm not going anywhere. I just like to walk around. I like to think."

"Well quit doing it. You're driving me crazy."

"All right!" she snapped, acting as if she were giving in, but knowing that she would work harder at not getting caught. Right now she told her father what he wanted to hear and thereby ended the conversation. She could get away from the table and escape. How humiliating. Even her own father thought she was capable of being somebody's secret lover. Nobody understood how truly pathetic she was.

The doorbell rang.

"That'll be for me," Big Joe said with finality. Then, with a peculiar reluctance in his gut, he got up from the table.

***

Vera let Lucas Cain into the foyer just as Evie was heading up the stairs.

"I have a meeting with Mr. Donovan," he said quietly.

There was something in the sound of the voice drifting up the stairway that made Evie turn around and look down at the stranger.

"Come in," Vera was saying, "Mr. Donovan's expecting you. He's in the front room. I'll take you to him."

Who is that, Evie wondered, very much in awe of the man's striking good looks. He was much older than she was, tall and dark. His tight-fitting white tee shirt showed off some impressive muscles, and his black trousers, that fit him to perfection, looked expensive.

Down in the foyer, Lucas could feel someone watching him, and this time he felt compelled to acknowledge the attention. He glanced up the stairs, and to his shock saw the vision of Clarice DuMaret Donovan alive again. Of course, he realized. This is incredible. She looks just like Clarice.

"Good lord," Evie sighed to herself, and turning hurried up the stairs, her belly fluttering. No one had ever looked at her that way before, with so much desire.

Vera led Lucas to the front room where Big Joe was waiting for him in his favorite chair. The calculated discomfort of the office in the city was nowhere present in Big Joe's home, but that was due mostly to the two hundred years of DuMaret hospitality that had been absorbed into the very woodwork. The house had its own innate way of making anyone feel welcome.

Lucas took a seat opposite Big Joe. He tried to maintain his cool and collected exterior, but the truth was he felt bewitched. "I think I saw your daughter just now on the stairs," he said. "She looks a lot like her mother, doesn't she?"

"Let me get one thing straight right now, Cain. You and I have a business relationship. My private life is private. Don't ever forget that. My daughter is off limits to everyone, and I don't want you discussing my late wife anymore, with anyone."

It was an unexpected request, but Lucas assured Big Joe that he would comply. Then he had trouble focusing on what Big Joe was saying for the rest of the evening. It felt surreal. He had always known Clarice gave birth before she died, yet he had never made the connection – that a part of Clarice had been here all the time quietly thriving in Solisville.

***

Evie paced the length of her stifling room, confounded by the fact that the stranger was right downstairs only one floor below her, but her father would have a fit if she disturbed a business meeting.

At last she decided on a plan of action. She pulled off her shorts and cotton shirt and slipped on a wispy sundress instead. She wanted to feel beautiful for a change. Finally, here was a man who excited her, and he had looked at her as though she was breathtaking? No one had ever looked at her like that before. Every cell of her body felt electrified.

She would slip down the backstairs, and then out the back door. Now more than ever she needed to get free. She needed some time to think about this. She hadn't been able to catch his name. How would she get her father to reveal it, to tell her who this man was, why he was in their home and more importantly, when he would be coming back again?

Outside, twilight was on the horizon and varying shades of dusk draped the world. A bright sliver of the summer moon could be seen just over the tops of the trees. The night seemed suitably magical and Evie felt an unfamiliar flutter of life opening inside her, down there between her legs.

She came around to the front of the house. In the driveway sat a black convertible with its top up. With a cautious curiosity, she approached the empty car.

He's still in the house, she assured herself. And what followed that thought was a peculiar thrill. A shot of excitement stabbed into her belly. Who is he, she wondered. He wasn't from Solisville, she was certain of that. She laid her hand on the hood of his car. It was still hot. She figured he had probably driven in all the way from New Orleans to meet with her father, but for what? What exactly did her father do, anyway? All she knew was that he went to work everyday and came home owning everything in town.

The porch light came on and Evie snapped to attention. The front door opened. Her father pushed open the screen door and stepped out onto the veranda followed by the handsome stranger. There was nowhere for her to hide. She was out in the open.

Big Joe saw her the minute he opened the screen door. "Evie," he called sharply, "come up here and get inside."

Lucas was startled to see her there as well. Evie, he thought to himself. At least this apparition has a name.

***

Lucas lay in bed and stared into the darkness of his hot room, dreaming awake. His eyes wide open, his hard-on once again in his fist, his mind was in another place, drifting…

Tonight, Big Joe had officially offered him a job with Donovan & Company, a sign that Lucas's success was genuine. It was something he'd worked for his entire adult life and now here it was, being handed to him. And yet all he could think about was Evie. How could he get to her without spoiling everything, without letting Donovan find out about it? He wanted to see Evie in the light, to hear her voice, to talk to her.

Lucas went at himself with fervor now, his mind filling with the promise of Evie.

There had been too many women in his experience, too many women that he'd ventured into sex with, and not one of them had lived up to his expectations. It had gotten to the point where he no longer even dated. His sex life had been reduced to the world in his head.

But now it's going to be different, he thought. All his other aspirations had come to pass, and this, too, was clearly his destiny.

The oppressive heat of his room nearly smothered him, but he continued to jerk himself off. His dream girl came readily to his imagination. Of course, now she looked suspiciously like Evie. At least her face did, the rest of her was pure fiction; a body that he hoped would be revealed to him in time. Meanwhile, he allowed her to look a little like Clarice, like how he remembered she'd looked, slender, pale as milk, with breasts that were full but subtle, nipples tiny and pink and tender seeming, a thatch of brown hair between her legs that hid the mystery of her sex.

Uncovering that particular mystery is what drove Lucas now. He wanted Evie's sex. He wanted to get between her legs. He tugged his cock more vigorously, becoming delirious. He knew women's bodies; he knew by heart what it would feel like. Her pussy would be tight but resilient with its slippery walls snug around his thickening hard-on as he pushed his cock into the depths of her. Her legs spread wide for him, he would pump into her hole with determination, until it accommodated him completely, until it stretched to receive the full length of him – until his cock was all the way in there and she was whimpering in his ear.

Up and down, with almost brutal consistency, Lucas tugged his dick in the privacy of his room.

Jesus, he was thinking, as every muscle in his body tensed in preparation for the climax, this is the one. He was going to be alone with her, he realized. Somehow she was going to be naked with him. She was going to be next to him, under him, on top of him. And it was going to happen soon, he knew it. He could feel it in his bones.

***

"I'm at the end of my rope with you!" Evie's father shouted.

He paced the foyer as Evie stood in silence on the stairs, afraid to move, afraid to speak, knowing her silence was only making his anger worse. "Are you losing your mind or just trying to make me lose mine? Whichever it is, Evie, you're doing a terrific job of it!"

She couldn't remember the last time she'd seen her father this angry. Still she refused to explain what she'd been doing out there, in one of her prettiest dresses. The longer her father shouted at her, the more she refused to speak. She was not going to let him spoil this.

***

Worn out from his tirade, Big Joe closed himself up in his suite of rooms and surrendered, calling it a night. At the bar in his study, he poured himself a snifter of cognac. Lingering over it, he paced slowly back and forth from one room to another, from the study to his bedroom and back again. He was feeling like he'd lost control, control over Evie, control over his instincts and over the past. How could he keep the past from overtaking the present? How could he shield Evie forever? It was wearing him out. He was tempted to give up, to let her run free, to let her make her own mistakes. Whatever it was she was doing, whomever it was she was seeing, he didn't seem able to control it, to stem the tide of trouble. Maybe it was simply her destiny to be just like her mother had been, running wild, carousing, being foolish and hedonistic. But he knew in his bones that Clarice would have wanted Evie to be different. He had to find the renewed strength to fight for her, for both of them.

But he was starting to feel old.

And now this development with Lucas Cain. Big Joe's intuition told him that Cain was good for the business, an asset all the way, professional, shrewd. Cain had figured out how to hide the fact that he was from the street. It ensured that Cain would work harder to stay at the top, for he had more to lose. But the mere fact that Cain was from the street was unsettling. He knew too much about Clarice. He had to make certain, somehow, that Lucas Cain stayed clear of Evie.

Something in his gut told Big Joe that Lucas Cain was a time bomb. Had he made a mistake in hiring him? He was usually so decisive. Why couldn't he make up his mind about this?

Evie undressed and got into bed. She wasn't going to push it tonight. She would stay in her room, but that didn't mean she would sleep. She was too excited.

He's going to come back, she told herself. Never had she been more certain of a thing in her life.

Chapter Six

The following evening, Big Joe stayed late at the office. A storm was in the air, one of those fleeting summer squalls. It would blow in a hurry and leave just as quickly. Evie was eager to embrace the fury of it; she didn't care if she got soaked. Everything about life now seemed made to order for her excitement.

She flew off the porch and down into the yard as the black clouds swooped in. All around her, the air had grown ominously still. A spatter of hard raindrops blew over the lawn, promising an immediate downpour. She stood in the center of it, in the same dress she'd worn the night before, feeling beautiful, feeling life, finally, swelling up inside her. Everywhere she looked, as the heavy rain let loose from the sky, life seemed to be reflecting her joy right back at her.

I'm crazy, she thought, her dress soaked and clinging to her, but she didn't care.

A great wind came then, following the rain, steadily pushing the storm past Solisville into the next county. Evie was drenched. She headed back toward the porch.

From out of nowhere, she saw him on the lawn. He seemed almost dream-like coming towards her with the mist lifting and the dusk falling. At first she wasn't positive it was him. He was in blue jeans and a black shirt, a pair of work boots, much less formal than he'd seemed the night before. She felt spooked. How did he get here, she wondered. Where's his car?

Lucas regarded Evie curiously. She was soaking wet. "You like the rain, I take it?" he observed with a friendly smile.

Evie was speechless.

He walked up to her. "I'm Lucas Cain," he said. "I was here last night to meet with your father."

Lucas Cain, she thought, letting the name tumble around in her brain. What was happening here? The dark was fast approaching, but she could still see well enough. Up close like this, he was almost too good looking. It intimidated her. His eyes were so dark and beautiful it made her nervous to look right at him. She'd never been this close to a man before, a man who had such magnetism. It was something masculine, a quality that seemed to radiate from him. "I remember you," she managed to say. "My father's not home right now. He's at his office."

"I know. I've just come from a meeting with him."

That was odd. "Did my father send you here?" she asked. "Does he need something?"

Lucas gauged the situation. Here she was as he'd hoped to find her, alone. What more could he ask for? He'd come this far. He might as well tell her the truth. "To be honest, Evie, your father wouldn't want me to be here at all. He wouldn't want me speaking with you. I already know that. That's why I parked my car up the road; I didn't want to draw attention to myself. I hope I'm not intruding, but I had to at least introduce myself. When I saw you last night, I couldn't believe my eyes. You look just like your mother."

Evie was stunned. "You knew my mother?"

"Yes," Lucas said. "Not very well, but I knew her."

"Is that why you were here last night, something to do with my mother?"

"No, I work for your father now. I work for Donovan & Company. That's why I was here."

Evie was intrigued. He worked for her father. That meant he would be around. "I didn't know my mother," she told him. "She died giving birth to me. But since you knew her, then I guess you know that."

He wasn't sure what to say to that. Could it be she actually believed the old story that Clarice had died giving birth to her? "Well, she was quite a woman, Evie. In fact, I've never met anyone else like her, which was why I was so startled to see you last night on the stairs. It felt like seeing a ghost."

"Well, you did look at me strangely," she said. "I guess now I know why." She felt like a perfect fool. Was that all it had been about? She reminded this man of her mother? How pathetic could she be? She should have known better than to think a man like him, obviously so much older, a man of experience, worldly even could want something from her. What use had he for someone as inexperienced as stupid Evie, who was standing there in a soaking wet dress with soaking wet hair?

"I would have introduced myself last night," he went on, "I really wanted to, but your father seems determined to keep his business life separate from his family. I don't suppose I blame him."

"He's pretty strict about it, all right. He drives me crazy with that sometimes. He's more than happy to arrange dates for me with hopelessly boring men from every other place on earth, but they better not be from Donovan & Company."

Lucas felt hopeful. Big Joe was still going to be an obstacle, but at least Evie sounded available. "He arranges dates for you?"

"Yes, he's trying to marry me off."

"But you're such a pretty young woman. I can't imagine you would need help with a thing like that. You must have more dates than you can handle."

"No, I don't." A tiny flame of hope ignited in Evie because he thought she was pretty. "The truth is I'm not very good at finding my own dates… men bore me to tears."

"Really? I hope I haven't been too tedious for you, then. I know it wasn't fair of me, dropping in on you like this."

She rushed to explain herself. "I didn't mean that you bored me. In fact, it's just the opposite. I mean, well…" She wanted to say he thrilled her. She wanted to say he made her feel excited and alive. She wanted to ask him to take her to bed, to take advantage of her, to teach her everything he knew about sex. She tried again. "You don't bore me at all," was all she could manage to say.

This was his opening. Lucas knew it. She might not be too articulate about it, but the woman was interested in him, he could tell.

"Evie," he said, "would you like to take a little walk with me?"

How exciting, a walk, alone. "I suppose I should change first. I'm soaked."

He looked at her clinging dress revealing all her perfect places. Her tiny nipples were rock hard. "I think you look great just as you are."

She knew what he was looking at; he was looking at her tits. It made her feel delirious. No one had ever looked at her with lust before. She was in over her head already but she didn't mind a bit. "I know every inch of this property," she told him. "I know it even in the dark. If you want, I can take you to a place where we can talk in private, where there's no one around."

"That sounds inviting," he said, and followed her through the overgrown thicket, back amidst the trees.

"I come out here a lot at night," she admitted. "Just to get out of my room, to get away from that awful house. It makes me nuts."

"How can you say that about such an incredible house? It has such history. Not to mention that it's worth a fortune."

"Well, if you were stuck there all your life, practically a prisoner, you might not feel that way. Out here at night, I can be myself. I can think about things."

They had reached the rock. They leaned against it. The trees overhead parted to reveal a now cloudless evening sky.

"What kind of things do you think about out here, Evie? If I'm not being too nosey."

"Well, for one thing, I think a lot about my mother. And, well, I think about other stuff, too." She wanted to get closer, to stand right next to him, to encourage him to touch her, maybe even kiss her, but she was too nervous to move.

"Evie, can I ask you something that's none of my business? Why is your father trying to marry you off?"

"It's an investment. I don't think he trusts me to have a life of my own. He wants me married to some businessman or other, to ensure my assets keep growing."

"But that's crazy, what about love?"

"That's what I want to know," she said quietly.

"I mean, at the very least, you'd think he'd want you to have the same shot at happiness that he had with your mother."

"Were they really that much in love? Did you know them well enough to know that for sure?"

"I think everybody knew it back then. They were very much in love."

"And I think maybe a little wild, too?"

Lucas thought that was an understatement, but the way she phrased it, with such naivety, charmed him. "Yes, Evie, I think they were a little wild."

"They went to motels and stuff."

"I guess so, yes. I suppose they did."

"Do you ever do that?" she asked.

"Do what?"

"Go to motels?"

"You mean, with women, to have sex?"

It shocked her a little that he was being so direct. But then what had she expected, that he wouldn't know about sex? "Yes, with women," her voice faltered, "to have sex."

"I did in the past," he told her honestly. "Once or twice. But I don't do that anymore. Why? Do you go to motels with men to have sex?"

"No. I've never been to a motel, for any reason." She looked up at him. He was so tall. She wanted to tell him the truth that she'd never had sex before. She'd never even come close. She was completely inexperienced, a virgin, hopelessly ignorant of everything. But she couldn't admit that. The conversation was going too well.

"I'm starting to get the impression that you never step foot off this property. You don't date much. You've never been to a motel…"

She laughed. "It's not that bad. I went to school up north for years. I go out to eat, I go shopping. I see movies. It's just that I don't, well, I don't do much that involves the opposite sex."

"Because men bore you," he added.

"No," she said. "Only the men I've known up until now."

He thought he understood what she was saying. She was sweet. "Evie," he asked her, "can I kiss you? I'd really like to kiss you right now."

It was what she had hoped for, yet she felt so unprepared. "I suppose so."

Lucas leaned down and kissed her on the lips, quickly, softly, keeping it harmless, keeping it tame. He wasn't sure where to go with her. Evie Donovan was not Clarice; she was from some other world.

Evie felt disappointed, and a little confused. Was that it? That was the kiss? Had he kissed her just to be polite? Even her own father could have kissed her like that. Was that the problem? Did Lucas think he was too old for her? "How old are you?" she asked him.

"I'm thirty-five, why? How old are you?"

"I'm almost twenty-two."

What was she trying to tell him, that she wasn't a child and wanted to be kissed? He took her in his arms this time and really kissed her, his tongue pushing in to explore her mouth.

Evie was overwhelmed by the suddenness of it. She was being kissed, her first real kiss. It was happening. She'd asked for it, and now what was she supposed to do? She put her arms around his neck. She kissed him back.

Lucas held her close to him while he kissed her, wet dress and all. Then he grabbed her ass and pulled her even closer, impossibly close, her soft breasts pushed up against his chest.

Evie's head was swimming. He was not only kissing her, he was actually touching her like she was made of flesh and blood and not money. He smelled incredibly good. It made her wish she'd had a chance to prepare for him, to have had an inkling he was coming. But he didn't seem a bit put off by her rain-soaked condition. He was clutching her wet dress now in his fists. The passion of his kiss increased and she could feel him lifting her dress back there; she could tell her panties were exposed. It thrilled her, not knowing what he was planning to do.

Then she became aware of what was happening to him. He'd gotten hard between his legs. He had an erection. She could feel his cock pressing up against her, rubbing her, bulging in his jeans. She knew this was a very good sign, that he liked kissing her.

His hands were under her dress now. The intensity of his kiss increased as he took her ass in his hands. She tried to keep up with his kisses, but things were happening quickly.

He'd slipped his hands up under her panties. His hands were touching her flesh, grabbing the flesh of her ass. And by the way he was groaning while he kissed her, it seemed to excite him a lot.

Then her panties were tugged down back there. It had happened so fast. He had tugged them a little down her thighs, enough to expose her entire bottom, and his hands were all over her rear end with even more enthusiasm than before. It made Evie wonder if her ass might be her most attractive feature.

Lucas felt delirious with lust, with pleasure. He found it hard to believe it was really happening. He hadn't expected her to be so willing, so compliant. He had barely kissed her and already she'd let her panties come down. His bulging cock ached in his jeans. He pushed it against her insistently. He couldn't wait for her to be naked, riding him, writhing around on him as she impaled herself on his cock. But he also wanted to savor this. He didn't want to rush past this part. It had been too long since he'd had a woman in his arms, and even then, he had never been with a woman who excited him like this. She smelled incredible. She smelled like rain, like the summer night, like warm flesh. He wanted to devour her.

He pulled the straps of her dress down her shoulders. He uncovered her tits and she let him do it, gasping sweetly as her flesh was exposed to the air. Her tiny nipples were very hard. Lucas sucked one into his mouth eagerly. He pulled on it with his lips, tormented it with his tongue. She sounded breathless. She was whimpering in his ear, clutching his hair. Her tits must be a favorite of hers, he thought. They must be very sensitive.

He pulled the other nipple lightly with his fingers. Women with sensitive breasts loved thorough and consistent pressure. He'd learned that; he knew that whatever attention he paid her here, now would leave her soaking between her legs.

He moved his mouth to her other nipple. He pulled and tugged and sucked it while her body writhed against his. She was clearly very excited. She was such a passionate lover.

Lucas unzipped his jeans to give his cock a little room.

Evie was delirious. She was too excited to think straight. It felt incredible what he was doing to her breasts. It made her want to be rid of her clothes. Impatiently, she slid the wet dress down her body, and then Lucas helped her pull it all the way off. To her shock, he fell to his knees in front of her. He pulled her panties farther down her thighs and then planted his mouth right on her, right down there, between her legs. His tongue slipped between the lips and licked her clitoris. Over and over he licked it, quickly, thoroughly, his tongue pressing up into it, pushing the clitoris in little circles.

The thrill was exquisite. It felt better than Evie could have ever imagined it would feel. Lucas pulled open the lips to expose her clitoris completely, and then his tongue went at her with renewed passion. If he kept this up much longer, she was going to come. She could feel it.

Lucas shoved Evie's panties all the down and she stepped out of them. Now he could really get his face in there. He pushed the lips open. They were engorged, soaking. "Spread your legs," he urged her quietly. "Get on my face."

Utterly bewildered, Evie spread her legs apart and Lucas pulled her more completely on to his face, centering her open pussy right on his mouth, his tongue licking her like mad. She was dripping all over him. She was too excited. She was straddling his face, clutching his head to steady her, to keep herself from falling over. And the more she ground herself down against the incredible sensation his mouth was creating in her, the more thoroughly his tongue licked her, the more intently his lips sucked her.

He slid his finger up her soaking hole.

"Oh God," she cried, accepting the finger, which was going in easily. She was bearing down on it. "God, oh, God," she whimpered.

Lucas had never felt anything so tight in his life. It can't be possible, he told himself. Then, with a sobering jolt, he realized it was very possible. In fact, judging by how protective Donovan was of Evie, and her comments about not dating many men, he knew it was not only possible that Evie was still a virgin, but highly probable.

He carefully slid his finger out of the tight hole.

"No," she cried. She'd been so close to coming. "Keep going!"

"Evie," he began, getting up from the ground and trying to pull himself together. "Can I ask you something?"

She already knew what he was going to say. She was mortified.

"Are you still a virgin?"

"Yes," she admitted. "But I don't want to be!"

Lucas was thunderstruck. It was one thing to defy Donovan and seek out Evie, fool around a little, maybe even progress to making love, becoming lovers, as he had hoped. But it was another matter entirely to deflower Big Joe Donovan's daughter. This was a good example of sex getting out of control. It was a thing Lucas had guarded against all his life, letting sex get the best of him, becoming his downfall. "Evie, I don't feel right about this," he explained. "I think we better re-think this. Maybe I'd better go."

"But it's okay," she pleaded with him. "I want to do this. I want you to do this. I want to be here with you, doing this."

"Evie, I think I'm too old for you. I don't think this is what's best for either one of us."

She cursed herself without mercy, and to make it worse, she began to cry.

The sight of her tears crushed him. "Evie, please, try to understand. It's not that I don't want to be with you. If it was as simple as that, if there was only you and me to think about, only here and now that mattered, it would be a different story. But there's your father to think of. He would kill me, and I wouldn't blame him."

Evie was devastated. Lucas was handing her her clothes. "Don't tell me you're afraid of my father," she blurted. She knew it was unkind, but she was impotent with rage.

"No," he said quietly. "I'm not afraid of your father. I'm afraid for myself. I have a career, Evie. I have dreams and aspirations, things that I've taken very seriously for many years. I don't want to risk destroying all that, everything I've built, by being foolish and acting in haste."

"So what are you saying," she sniffed, "that you want time to think, is that it?"

"I guess so, Evie. I guess that's it."

Chapter Seven

Lucas Cain rose to the challenge of Donovan & Company. Within a matter of days he'd learned the ropes. He knew who was who and what each person was responsible for.

Donovan & Company wasn't just about selling real estate and sometimes buying it; it was about building the real estate in the first place. It was about knowing the territory, who was doing what, when and where, and getting there first. It was about keeping everything up to code. It was about keeping Donovan up to speed about who was looking for graft. It was about local politics in Solisville and utilizing Donovan's television station to keep the political climate swayed in his favor. It was about staying on top of what news, or rumors, were making it into The Evening Call.

Big Joe seemed satisfied with Lucas's early progress. He forgot about his misgivings. He congratulated himself on having known when it was time to unload Bert Hannon and take on some new blood. Everywhere Cain went, people were impressed, and that only reflected positively on Big Joe's lavish empire.

There was plenty of entertaining to do, too. And Big Joe expected Lucas to be on hand at every occasion, in fancy restaurants and in people's homes, especially if there were women present. Lucas Cain was always a hit with wives and daughters.

After hours, though, Lucas went home alone. Those fleeting hours in the night were fast becoming the only time Lucas was even in his own house. He'd hired a cleaning service to come in each day and keep his house spotless, his laundry washed and pressed and his sheets immaculately clean. He never saw the cleaning service. He came in each night and everything was as it was supposed to be, almost as if nobody lived there, as if no one were ever at home.

His nights hadn't changed. Lucas went to bed alone, his cock in his fist, images of his dream girl surging up to the forefront of his imagination as the dark honed in on him, as the relentless heat enveloped him. But the thing that had changed, that had seemed to change permanently, was that Clarice DuMaret Donovan was gone now.

As much as he tried to summon her, the woman that came into his imagination instead was always Evie. And as much as he tried to resist the lewd thoughts that were in his head, he couldn't. They were too compelling. He had loved being with her, even though it had been fleeting and had ended badly. He couldn't resist taking the trip back there in his mind. Like clockwork, he did it every night. The images rose in his head and before too long he gave his lust over to them. He fucked Evie thoroughly and hard, in every imaginable position.

Chapter Eight

The hot summer days dragged on and every morning found Evie on her front porch endlessly waiting, certain that Lucas Cain would return. For hours each day, she waited. Now she truly felt like a restless lover needing to be rescued from all the searing agony of desire. Why did she have to be such a little fool? She couldn't figure herself out. It's not as if she could have unloaded her virginity onto someone else and been different for Lucas. There simply hadn't been anyone else. No one had even seemed motivated enough to kiss her before.

The only thing in her life more unbearable than the endless days were the hot, tortuous nights. She had taken to waiting until after midnight before slipping out of the house. Now more than ever she couldn't stand being alone in her room, in her suffocating bed. And it was imperative that her father not catch her leaving. Under no circumstances could she afford to be followed, because every night now Evie stood completely naked out there beneath the trees. Her legs spread wide under the black sky, she was driving herself crazy with lust. Orgasm after orgasm would overtake her as she succumbed to the memories of what it had been like to be with Lucas Cain, the things he'd done to her, the way he'd made her body feel.

To make the situation worse, once a week now, without fail, the Donovan dinner table was graced with the presence of Cal Harper. He was practically becoming a fixture in the Donovan household. Evie's father was pushing her on Cal with very little subtly, and to his admirable credit, Cal was gracious and seemed eager to take her on.

Her father had been right, although Evie was reluctant to admit it. Cal Harper wasn't a bad sort. He'd been educated at Harvard and he'd traveled extensively in Europe. He found things to talk about besides Evie's money, or even his own money, for that matter. Physically, he wasn't unattractive, and there was something about him, a civility that made him easy to be with. She had even left the house with him on one occasion and gone to a cocktail lounge with him. Cal had a way about him, a way of making her feel at ease. He'd even kissed her while they'd sat in the front seat of his car, and she had reciprocated willingly. They touched tongues for a few uneasy moments, but then Evie pulled away discreetly.

When Cal's hand had moved to caress her breast, his fingers straying lightly across the fabric of her shirt, she didn't say no. His touch wasn't intrusive. He stroked her breasts until the nipples were erect and she was breathing heavily. But when he asked for permission to lift her shirt, to touch her, flesh-to-flesh, she resisted again. She said no.

The truth was Evie was afraid of Cal. Was she afraid of getting used to him, of liking him too much? Or maybe just settling for him because Lucas still hadn't come back to her?

She hated to admit it to herself, but deep down she knew that if Cal had pressured her just a bit more that night in his car, she would have agreed. She was raw with lust. She would have let Cal Harper lift her shirt and touch her breasts, and God only knew what else. She'd even masturbated one night wondering about Cal, what it might feel like to have sex with him; to let him be the one to finally do the deed, to let him be the one to have intercourse with her and maybe disgrace her in all sorts of lurid ways right there in the front seat of his car.

After the orgasm had ripped through her, showing Evie to herself too clearly, she had felt a little sick to her stomach. Who did she think she was? How could she even consider letting another man touch her, arouse her, expose her, use her, when she knew she was in love with Lucas Cain?

The next time Cal Harper was seated at the Donovan's dining room table, Evie felt a little ashamed. She found it hard to look him in the eye.

***

Everything seemed to be working out fine, Big Joe thought. Finally, he had a little peace of mind. Evie had stopped sneaking out at night, and she seemed to genuinely like Cal Harper. And it was easy enough for anyone to see that Cal was wild about Evie.

It was too soon to push for an engagement, but it was time for one of Big Joe's extravaganzas. Twice a year he spared no expense and entertained at the mansion. Once at Christmas and then in late summer, when the people in town were ready for a vacation, ready for any excuse to forget about work; to stay out late while the days were longer, to drink free booze and dance a little under the stars.

For the first time in a long time, Big Joe could almost say he felt happy. He'd made so many mistakes in his life, and though he knew nothing could ever fix what had happened to Clarice, at least he'd somehow managed to save Evie. She'd gone through a rough and restless patch, but she was going to be all right now. Big Joe felt certain of it.

He'd insisted she find herself the prettiest dress she could for the party. She was, after all, the richest woman in Solisville now, and one day the mansion, and pretty much the whole town, would pass to her. It was time she started living up to that image; give the people in town a little bit of what they wanted, of what they came out to the mansion for, pomp and circumstance and the trappings of obvious wealth.

When Evie had agreed, Vera was delighted and Big Joe was relieved. Evie made an entrance that night that left everyone breathless, not only Cal Harper – whose proud feathers puffed out – but especially Big Joe. It's Clarice, he realized, as Evie came down those stairs in a strapless gown, her hair pulled up and her face luminous. To keep his heart from breaking, Big Joe turned his thoughts to business. Had anyone arrived yet that he could talk shop with?

This was the night Evie had been waiting for all summer. It was the night she knew she'd finally see Lucas Cain again. No one employed by Donovan & Company would risk offending her father by not showing up at his gala. She did everything she could to make an impression that she felt would knock Lucas off his feet, resorting to that time-honored feminine wile of turning herself into living bait.

"You look so beautiful, Evie," Cal said in awe. And he said it with such sincerity that it made her feel a pang of regret. She knew it was only a matter of time and Cal was going to ask her to marry him. She had no desire to hurt him, but she couldn't imagine herself saying yes.

Cal had driven in from New Orleans with his father to attend the party. It was a long way to come, even though he'd known that Evie would need to circulate, that he wasn't necessarily her date. In fact, she had made certain that Cal understood she was a free agent. She felt guilty enough about being deceitful, or at best evasive, about her intentions toward him. She thought the least she could do was spare him the feeling that he'd been publicly jilted if he turned around during the party and discovered that she was gone.

And Evie had every intention of disappearing. As soon as she could get him alone, she wanted to talk with Lucas. And with any luck, do a lot more than talk. She wanted to be one of those girls who returned to the center of a party with her hair slightly mussed and her lipstick smeared. And nobody would ever know who had been the lucky fellow.

Outside an orchestra was playing. A dance floor had been set up just off the patio, the patio having been turned into one of the many open bars. On the sprawling back lawn tents had been erected that held enough tables and chairs, it seemed, to seat the population of Solisville.

It was a perfect night, warm enough to remind everyone that it was late summer, but for August in Louisiana, it wasn't unbearable. Tiki torches dotted the yard to keep the endless mosquitoes at bay. The feeling in the air was festive. Of course, it was still early and no one had had a chance yet to drink too much, but that would come later. It always did at these affairs.

Cal Harper looked dapper in his white dinner jacket with

every hair in place. From his black bow tie to his shiny black shoes, Cal Harper looked like money. The understated smell of the Ivy League was all over him.

Evie met Cal's father for the first time. It was a perfect night for the introduction. Big Joe was beaming as he introduced his daughter to the potential father-in-law, and it was clear to Evie from the twinkle in Mr. Harper's eye that he viewed her as a merger made in heaven. What father wouldn't want his son to be the heir to the town of Solisville? That would be prize enough, but for the wife to be as stunning as Evie, well, that was just icing on the lovely cake.

To Big Joe's continued delight and amazement, Evie circulated amongst the guests seeming to know by instinct which people it would be particularly prudent to cater to. She even agreed to dance with several of them, a thing Big Joe had never seen. In fact, he was pleasantly surprised that his daughter even knew how to dance. He chalked it up to the boarding school up north. It was money well spent, he thought with satisfaction.

The local celebrities were in attendance, specifically the two news anchors from Big Joe's television station. They caused a general buzz wherever they went. And Susie, the reporter from The Evening Call's society page, was there with her photographer in tow. She was a fixture at any local social function. The less affluent and, therefore, overly ambitious of the Solisville wives vied all evening for Susie's attention. For those with no higher aim in life, it was a coveted honor to have one's picture appear in the society column of The Evening Call, especially when the column was devoted to a Donovan gala.

Food was everywhere in abundance that night, the old DuMaret kitchen having been overrun by an army of darting white coats from the Petit Maison Blanc catering company.

Outdoors, the serving tables were laid with eye-popping displays, and waiters carrying finger foods on silver trays slipped in among the growing crowds.

When the orchestra dove into the lush opening strains of the old romantic standard, You Belong to Me, Evie couldn't believe her eyes. Lucas Cain emerged from the crowded patio dressed impeccably in a sleek tuxedo, a half-empty champagne glass in his hand. He was engrossed in conversation with Evie's father and another man, and the women in the immediate area parted in a sea of awe as Lucas moved obliviously through them.

Her heart racing, Evie politely excused herself from the mindless repartee of a local stuffed shirt who was too full of his own importance. She went right over to her father. "I don't think we've met," she said graciously, offering her hand to Lucas.

Lucas took her hand and calmly looked her in the eye.

"This is Lucas Cain, Evie," her father said. "He works for me, primarily out of New Orleans."

"It's nice to meet you, Mr. Cain. I'm glad you could come."

"I wouldn't have missed it for the world," he replied, letting go of her hand. He smiled politely and tried hard not to let it show in his face how beautiful he thought she looked. It was Clarice again, only more breathtaking now.

"Don't tell me you've come alone, Mr. Cain? This isn't a night for business, you know. This is a night to be festive, to leave your work at the office." She turned to her father. "Did you forget to tell him about that?"

"Cain never stops working," her father put in good-naturedly.

"Besides, when you come alone," the other man joked, "it's that much easier to leave with a little unexpected dessert. Isn't that right, Cain?"

"That's right," Lucas agreed flatly.

Evie searched his face for a hint of recognition, anything to indicate he was alive under that cool exterior. She didn't want to push her luck. She was getting a clear signal from her father that she should move on, that business was being conducted. She made a bold move before leaving, though. "Do you dance, Mr. Cain?" she asked. "I'd be happy to take a quick spin around the floor with you later, if you'd like. Come look for me, I'll be around." Without stopping to take in the expression on her father's face, she quickly departed from the trio, her heart pounding. There was nothing out of line about that, she convinced herself. Everything about it was in perfect keeping with how she'd behaved all evening. A setup, that's what it had been. The entire evening so far had been a setup for just that moment, that moment when Lucas Cain came into view. Now all she could do was wait. How long would it be before Lucas took the bait?

She mingled half-heartedly throughout the evening, always with a distracted eye scanning the crowded party for Lucas. And without fail, Lucas was always at the side of her father.

If he wanted to get away, he would. The last thing she had ever considered was that Lucas would keep himself unavailable, regardless of how tempting she'd made the bait.

She mindlessly nibbled on the extravagant food, but none of it appealed to her; it all seemed tasteless. She accepted several invitations to dance, but only in hopes that seeing her on the dance floor would prod Lucas to take a turn with her. She avoided the crush at the bars altogether. She was too depressed now to add alcohol to the mix. When a waiter approached her with two delicate glasses of champagne on a silver tray, her first thought was to send him away. But before she could so much as shake her head, a man smoothly lifted both glasses from the waiter's tray, handing one of them to her. It was Lucas Cain.

"You looked like you could use a little pick-me-up," he said. "I told your father I was coming over here to re-charge your battery. Appearances are everything to a crowd like this and you are the hostess, after all."

"Lucas," she sighed quietly.

"I can't stay long. Your father's watching us. You look stunning," he added under his breath.

"Dance with me," she pleaded.

"Evie, I can't."

"Meet me somewhere, then. Somewhere no on will see us. I want to talk with you. I've been waiting all summer for this."

"Evie—"

"Lucas, please."

"But I can't."

"You can find a way, I know you can. You can disappear into the crowd and meet with me, even for a few minutes."

"Drink your champagne, Evie," he said. "Your father's watching us."

They lightly touched glasses and she obediently sipped her champagne.

"I'll try to get away," he said finally. "Evie, you know this could be a disaster."

"But it won't be, I promise. I just want to talk with you."

"Where should we meet? We can't go where we were last time. We'll never get off the lawn with this many people around."

"Go into the house, then," she said. "Go up the backstairs. Meet me in my room. It's halfway down the hall on the right."

"Your room?" For the first time all evening, Lucas nearly lost his composure. "Evie, that sounds like your worst idea yet."

"But no one would dream of going up to my room, all the bars are down here," she insisted.

"Then how will I explain why I'm doing it?"

"No one will notice you. The house is in chaos with the catering company. Please, Lucas."

He drank his champagne. He scanned the crowd for Evie's father. "I'd better go now," he said.

"Lucas, please."

"Okay," he agreed. "I'll try. Give me twenty minutes."

Chapter Nine

With almost uncontrollable anticipation, Evie waited for Lucas in her room. The lights off, she sat as near to the window as she dared and watched the many partygoers outside on the lawn. Everyone seemed to be having an enchanted evening, they truly did. The compelling music the orchestra played filled the air, and in addition to the torches burning brightly at the edges of the lawn, there were at least a hundred flickering votive candles dotting the night.

Evie tried to pick Lucas out from the throng, but she couldn't see him anywhere. Perhaps that meant he was already on his way.

A thrill shot through her belly. What was she getting herself into? Lucas Cain in her bedroom? She'd never dreamed she could be so bold.

Her ears strained for the slightest sound on the stairs or in the hallway. She'd left her bedroom door partially open, but now she feared Lucas might wander the hallway in search of the right room, wasting precious time. She moved closer to the door.

At last she saw him. He had found his way up the backstairs. God, he looked incredible. The tuxedo only made him look more handsome and she wouldn't have thought that was possible. Quickly, she stepped into the light. "Over here," she whispered.

Lucas saw her.

What am I doing, he asked himself. Am I crazy? But look at her; she's so beautiful. And that dress...

He slipped into her room. "Hello, Evie," he whispered back, pushing the door closed quietly behind him. Then he took her in his arms and kissed her. A real kiss. He wouldn't make the same mistake twice.

Evie felt overwhelmed by her excitement. She tried to get hold of herself. Most of all, she didn't want to lose control of herself or the situation. She didn't want anything to happen that could lead her to tears, to humiliating herself in front of him again.

She let him kiss her for as long as he wanted to, their bodies becoming impossibly close. She wanted to hurry him along. She wanted to step out of her dress. But she resigned herself to being slowly kissed, to feeling the sensation of the hard-on that was rising inside his trousers press insistently against her mound. She was simply going to have to be patient somehow.

Being here with him like this, in his arms again, she knew there was no mistaking that he was the one she wanted, the one she wanted for her lover. She was not going to settle for anything less, not for Cal Harper or anyone else. It didn't matter that Lucas worked for her father. She wouldn't let it matter. It didn't matter that he was so much older than her, so much more experienced. That could only work in her favor, she decided.

"Evie," Lucas whispered, "you know I can't stay long. Eventually my absence, and yours, too, is going to be noticed."

"I know."

"What was it you wanted to talk to me about?"

"Nothing," she confessed, "just this. I just wanted this. I wanted to talk to you about how much I missed you and how I want to be with you like this."

"Evie, you know it's not a good idea."

"I don't care!"

"Hush, keep your voice down."

She lowered her voice to a whisper again. "But it's true, I don't care." She kissed him again, holding him closer to her, hoping with all her heart that he would make love to her right there and then and quench the burning desire that had become so constant, so tormenting. She urged him over towards her bed.

"Evie, no," he said firmly.

She parted the mosquito netting. "Sit with me," she whispered, "just for a little while. No one could possibly know we're gone yet, no one will come in here."

Against his better judgment – was it the champagne? – Lucas sat down with her on the bed.

Evie lowered the top of her strapless gown. Her bare breasts, as pale as they were, seemed luminous in the dark.

"Evie, we can't, not here, not like this. There are hundreds of people downstairs." Still, he was caught by the vision of her perfect tits; the gentle weight of them exposed, ready for him, waiting for his mouth to suck the tender nipples. He knew it was what he wanted. How could he resist it when she was offering them so freely?

Her nipple was between his lips and he sucked it insistently, before he knew what he was even doing. The way she gasped, the sheer delight that seemed to shoot through her whole body when his lips touched her, only increased his feeling of urgency. It really was what he wanted after all, to be with her again like this. To deny it would be pointless.

He didn't know how far he could take her, or should take her, but right now he didn't care. He caressed her breasts with his hands, his mouth, his tongue. His ears filled with the sweet erotic sound of her obvious pleasure and he felt intoxicated. His aching cock strained against the fly of his expensive trousers.

Jesus, he cursed himself. His lust was overtaking him. He was having trouble taking it slow.

Evie had unzipped her gown, and now she peeled the length of it away. She was wearing nothing now but a pair of diamond earrings, a tiny satin thong, and a pair of high-heeled sandals.

This was an even more captivating creature than the drenched kitten he had been with earlier that summer. In fact, he couldn't believe his good fortune. She was so exquisite, and she was offering herself to him.

She lay back on the bed and Lucas leaned over her to kiss her again, his tongue pushing into her eager mouth while his hand explored the satin thong. She parted her legs for him, and he quickly discovered that the delicate strip of satin between her legs was soaking wet.

Evie moaned. His warm hands were on her, finally! His fingers trailed enticingly over her mound, between her legs, up her thighs. The promise of being touched there again, of being probed, caressed, devoured, of having her swollen, tender clitoris once again held captive by his merciless tongue, made her kiss him more deeply; her moans growing more full of passion. The sound, the sensation of her own arousal overwhelmed her.

He slid his fingers up under the damp thong and this time, to his surprise, he discovered that the lips down there were smooth. She was shaved. Oh God, she's too perfect, he thought. Then he couldn't help himself. He stripped down her thong, tugging it free of her ankles, and pushed her legs apart.

What a vision it was. Without hair down there, she seemed so impossibly naked, the smooth, pouting mound revealing all its folds. He wished he could turn on the lights, feast his eyes on this deliciously bare pussy spread out before him, but he didn't dare risk turning on a light. He hadn't completely lost his mind, not yet.

Recklessly kneeling on the floor in his tuxedo, Lucas planted himself between her thighs. He kissed the slick swollen pussy lips, his tongue licking the length of them from her clitoris to her hole. She smelled like perfume, like soap, like pussy, all of it at once. His nose took in that smell and his mind reeled. He sucked the lips now almost ferociously; he honed in on her clitoris and sucked mercilessly on it, too.

She gasped, she cried out, she whimpered. She clutched the blankets, digging her fingers in. She thrust her pussy out wide. His mouth was so warm, so wet, his tongue relentless. Her clitoris was clamped between his lips and his tongue licked the tiny hood, circling it, and then licking it again.

Then, while his hands pushed her lips more completely open, his tongue licked around the opening of her hole. Around and around the tongue licked, her abandoned clitoris now engorged and throbbing. She was delirious in this wave of mounting desire. She'd never felt anything so erotic. His tongue continued to circle her tight hole, his fingers pulling it more gently open, until she felt certain his tongue was actually in her, had entered her. He was probing into that tight soaking slot of hers with his tongue and the penetration, the pressure of it, felt incredible.

In and out his tongue moved, rhythmically, his hands keeping her spread wide, keeping her hole open, letting the tongue work its way into her. When her hole was relaxed, pushing out, his tongue swirled around in the inner opening. She could feel it in there. She grabbed onto her thighs to spread herself more, if that were even possible. She offered herself up to him. She bore down on his tongue.

Then his mouth went back to attending her clitoris. Now he was easing a finger up inside her, and it was sliding easily into her hole while he licked her. She was certain it was all the way in. The finger was moving in and out of her.

God, she was going to come like this, his attention to her clitoris was too acute, but she was trying with all her strength to stave it off, to make this thrilling sensation last. The finger was going all the way in her and rubbing her in there.

She hiked her hips up to meet the depth of the probing finger. The way it rubbed her inside with his tongue licking her clitoris so thoroughly made her bear down on him with all her strength. And as she did that – as her hips bucked up to meet him and she held her thighs wide – a second finger went into her and it didn't hurt she was that open.

Would he fuck her now, she wondered. She was so obviously ready for him. "God, Lucas," she cried in her delirium, "please do it, fuck me. I really want you to fuck me!"

But he was too encumbered by the tuxedo, the jacket, the vest, the studs and the cummerbund. All of it would have to go before he could even get his trousers down. He didn't want to be that reckless. It was better to just keep doing this. Besides, he was enjoying every moment of it. He eased the two fingers into her hole as deep as they would go. He eased them out again, and let up on her clitoris. His tongue circled around it now, no longer licking across the hood of it, just teasing it as his fingers eased back up into her hole. The extreme tightness was easing up, the hymen was stretching. She didn't seem to be in any pain.

He slid his fingers deeper into her, found that spot up inside her and rubbed it hard, giving it all he had as his lips sucked directly on her clit, shoving her into ecstasy.

An orgasm like nothing she'd ever felt tore through Evie. Nothing, nothing at all, had ever been that deep inside of her, had ever moved around in her. Her legs shook, her whole body jerked as wave after wave of intense pleasure exploded in her muscles, pushing the fluids out of her. Evie's orgasm spurted out and drenched Lucas's face.

She was too breathless to speak. She lay there spread open and panting, still clutching her thighs. "Oh my God," was all she could manage to say.

Lucas's knees ached and his hard-on was killing him. His face was a mess. "Evie, honey," he said, "where's the bathroom?"

Alone in there with the door closed, at last he unzipped his fly. He freed his cock from the folds of its prison, and he jerked himself off into the toilet bowl.

He came quietly, soundlessly. He didn't want her to guess what he was doing. He steadied himself against the wall with his free hand and let the searing hot ecstasy of his come shoot out of him, spurt after spurt after spurt.

My God, she was incredible. He'd never done anything like that. He'd never been with a virgin before... a final spurt of his come shot out and down into the water.

"I'm going to have her," he said, fixing his hair in the mirror, cleaning his face, straightening his bow tie. Next time, he promised himself, his cock was going to come out and play.

By the time Lucas returned to the bedroom, Evie had managed to pull herself together. Well, at least her dress was on.

"I'd better get back to the party," he said. "We've been gone for too long."

"I know," she agreed with regret. "I'm going to fix my face now. Lucas," she said as he was heading for the door. "When can I see you again?"

He sighed. "Evie, I don't know."

"But you want to see me again, don't you?"

"I sure do, honey. I really do."

"We can meet out there by that rock anytime. I can always meet you there after dark. Just tell me, get word to me somehow and I'll be waiting for you."

"I will, Evie."

"You promise?"

"I promise," he said as he let himself out.

***

Evie had gotten her wish; she'd gotten what she'd planned for all summer. But she decided it was too risky to return to the party with her hair mussed and her make-up smeared, so she fixed herself in the bathroom mirror.

She looked stunning. She glowed. Her face was more luminous than before. She still felt delirious. In honor of that, of her secret, of the time spent with her new lover's face between her legs, she went back to her father's party without wearing her panties. And she danced with many men until late into the night, her smooth, slick lips hiding underneath her gown, naked and still a little swollen.

Chapter Ten

It was a week later when Evie heard from Lucas Cain, a week that had passed as slowly as a year. And during that year-long week there had been another dinner with Cal Harper. He'd been particularly excited to be with Evie again after the astounding impression she'd made on every man at the party. Evie had tried hard to keep a cool distance in her voice all during dinner to keep him from being too hopeful about her, but she had trouble negotiating that fine line between sparing Cal's feelings and being outright rude.

Big Joe wondered to himself if perhaps they'd had a fight, but he kept out of it.

When Lucas finally telephoned Evie, it was in the middle of the day. He was at a restaurant in Solisville, entertaining clients with Big Joe. He'd excused himself briefly to use the phone, knowing for sure that with Big Joe left sitting at the table, he couldn't possibly be at home.

Luckily, Evie had answered the phone when it rang and not Vera.

"I can see you tonight," he said quickly. "Shall I meet you there?"

"If you think you can find your way. Otherwise, I can wait for you where the lawn ends just inside the trees."

"Okay, wait there."

"What time?" she asked hurriedly.

"Around midnight. I should be free by then. I have a long day ahead of me."

"I'll be there," she said. Then she hung up the phone.

***

It was midnight when Big Joe came home. Even though she knew her father was still awake, Evie had no time to lose. She managed to slip down the backstairs and out the back door without being detected. She hurried across the lawn.

To her delight, Lucas was waiting for her. As always, he looked more handsome than she remembered. It took her breath away. "I'm sorry I'm late,' she apologized. My father came home when I was on my way out. I had to be careful."

"I know," Lucas said. "I had the same trouble. I've been following his damn car all the way here."

"Where is your car?"

"I left it up the road. Don't worry. I won't take any chances. I'm sure I have more to lose than you do if we get caught. I'm not going to let it happen."

Evie wondered if she should kiss him. Then she decided it would be best if they moved a little farther from the house. When they were hidden amongst the trees, she turned to face him. He smelled so good. "I missed you," she said.

"I missed you, too."

He kept it casual, but it was an understatement. He had missed her incredibly. Never had he been so sexually obsessed with a woman in his life.

"Did you really miss me?"

"Yes, Evie, I really did. I'm not just saying that."

She put her arms around him then and kissed him. She was surprised to discover that he was already hard. She pulled quickly away from him. It was too intimidating, that hard-on. She wasn't ready for it yet. She led him deeper into the trees, over to the rock, her sanctuary.

That cock of his was too challenging, an utter mystery that no one had ever cared enough to explain to her. "I wish we could be in my room again," she said nervously, for lack of anything else to say. "That was fun."

Lucas didn't reply. He didn't need to make small talk. He took her in his arms and resumed the kiss, pressing his erection up against her.

Evie worried that tonight more would be expected of her. She was afraid of disappointing him. The other night had been perfect. She wanted to re-live it, yet she also wanted to surpass it for his sake. But how? She was so inexperienced at this. How did other people ever figure this sex stuff out?

"What's the matter, Evie?" Lucas asked. "What's on your mind?"

"Nothing," she lied.

"Something's on your mind, I can tell. You're distracted."

"I just want to please you," she confessed. "And I don't have a clue what I'm doing."

"Of course you do," he assured her. "You're doing just fine."

She let herself be kissed again. His seeming confidence in her was giving her courage. She let one of her hands go down to his legs, to the front of his trousers where his erection was straining.

He took her face in his hands and kissed her more passionately, groaning audibly as she timidly caressed his pants.

His obvious approval fueled her to be bolder. She touched him more firmly there, until she was practically groping him.

"I'll help you," he said, unzipping his pants. "Here," he told her when his cock was free, "this is better."

A little in awe, Evie touched it. His cock was thick and firm and hot. It stood straight out from his fly, rigid and stiff.

Lucas put his hand firmly around Evie's and showed her how to pump the skin back and forth, back and forth, pulling the skin clear up to the head of his cock. "I'm not circumcised," he explained to her. "When you pull the skin up like this, it feels incredible. When you pull it back like this," he showed her, "it feels even better." He let go of her hand, giving her some room to experiment. Her inexperience made her clumsy, but her clumsiness was cute. It perplexed him and aroused him at the same time. He was used to his own rhythm, his own fist. It felt good to be touched by her. When was the last time he was with a woman who had touched him like this? But he was never going to come this way. After a time, he motioned for her to stop and tucked himself back in his trousers.

She was disappointed. "Are we finished?" She felt she had failed him.

"No." He smiled warmly at her. "I just don't want to rush it. There's no hurry, is there?"

"I suppose not. Lucas, can I ask you something? I've been thinking about it a lot."

"What's that?"

"Do you date other women? Are you seeing anyone else?"

"No, Evie," he said. "And I shouldn't even be seeing you."

"You know what I was thinking?"

"What?"

"I was thinking that if you lived alone..." She suddenly felt embarrassed. She was pushing herself on him.

"We wouldn't have to meet so late at night, in the middle of nowhere?"

"Yes."

"Evie, I live clear in New Orleans and I usually work very late. How would we explain that? You could easily be out all night if you came home with me."

But clearly Evie had been giving the scenario some consideration, considering whatever various outcomes might arise. "Then we could go to a motel," she offered. Just the word 'motel' coming out of her mouth excited her. They could be alone together, naked in the same bed, with no fear of getting caught or getting found out. It would be so liberating that she got wet just thinking about it.

Lucas was surprised by her suggestion and by where her private thoughts were taking her. "And what motel could we go to around here where they wouldn't recognize us, or you, at the very least?"

"There must be someplace between here and New Orleans where no one would know us."

He studied her face, her perfectly sincere, eager eyes. He thought of what she was offering him. He wondered what it would be like to be her first. Would he have the patience for her inexperience? Would he be too excited to take his time with her? He knew he wanted to fuck her. That much he knew without a doubt. But in his fantasies she was experienced and able to meet his needs. What would reality be like? Probably a challenge.

Well, if that's what it takes to be with her, he decided, then that's what it takes. "All right," he promised her at last. "The next time I have a few hours free, we'll find a motel. We will. I'll take you there. We'll make love in the middle of the afternoon. Does that sound good?"

Evie was ecstatic. Finally, her virginity was as good as gone. He was telling her that he was going to be the one. "Thank you, Lucas." She pulled him up close again and they kissed. And this time their kiss unleashed the tidal wave. Their politeness with each other was gone; their hesitancy was over. They forgot about time, and where they were, and how they were supposed to behave.

She wasn't afraid of his erection now. She pressed right up against it while they kissed, letting her mound rub his cock, suggestively inviting him to do it now, to fuck her right here in the open. She knew that he wouldn't do it, she was only playing, but she rubbed against him anyway.

Boldly, she unzipped his trousers. Lucas helped her bring his swelling cock out into the air again by shoving his pants and his briefs down his thighs. He was very hairy there around his stomach and thighs. His cock sprang straight up from a mass of coal-black curls. He was the first grown man Evie had ever seen with his pants down. She was wishing there was more than just moonlight to see him by.

She slipped her hands up beneath her dress and tugged her panties down, kicking them free, not caring if she found them or not when it was time to leave.

She lifted her skirt so he could see her again, her perfectly smooth mound that was already dripping, her tender lips swelling, eager to be caressed.

He, too, wished he could really see her as he lightly ran a finger over her pouting sex lips. He felt the nub of her clitoris protruding from between them. The lips felt slick. He knew she was very wet. He crouched down, leaning against the rock. He pulled her hips up close to him, planting his mouth right on her mound. Her ass cheeks filled his hands and he kept her pressed there, close to his face, his tongue darting in and tormenting her clitoris.

Evie rocked herself against his tongue. Losing her balance, she leaned over him to steady herself against the rock. But then her dress tumbled down around his head. She pulled it up and off her completely. She was naked now except for the sneakers on her feet.

He pulled her up onto his face, until she was straddling him. He'd done this to her before, when they were out here like this the first time, but now she felt braver. Grasping the rock, she really parted her legs for him this time. Lewdly, she mashed her spread pussy against his mouth, encouraging his tongue to be thorough and relentless, to devour her until she couldn't stand it. "Put your fingers in me like you did before," she pleaded. "I want to feel it. I want to feel filled up."

He groaned deliriously into her pussy while he sucked it, smothering in the slippery folds of it. The thought of filling her, of really filling her, was making him crazy. His stiff cock was throbbing, aching to be relieved.

He slid a cautious finger up her slippery hole and it went in easily. He tried two. It was tight, but she didn't complain. She moaned. She worked herself on his fingers then, bearing down, squirming on them. And what it suggested to his lurid imagination as she squatted over his face impaled on his fingers was almost more than he could stand. "Evie," he gasped. "I need to get up."

He stood, and to her surprise, he asked her to bend over, to push herself out for him. He wanted to lick her from behind.

This sounded really dirty to Evie, so she did it eagerly.

In an instant he was down again between her legs, licking her, sucking her. The feeling made her bend over even further, made her spread her legs wider and push her ass out.

He jerked himself off while he licked her. He probed his tongue into her tight hole over and over, coming back to that hole, that hole that was keeping them from really knowing pleasure.

Letting go of his cock, he focused on getting her tight hole to open. He pulled the lips wide, he coaxed the opening with his tongue, caressing it with licks and nibbles and sucks. Suggestively, he fucked the confounding hole with his tongue. He slid a finger in again, carefully, methodically, and then he slid in two. The hole was being cooperative and Evie sounded like she was in ecstasy.

They were making progress. "Push yourself against my fingers," he encouraged her, "like you were doing before."

She felt hopelessly dirty like this, and she loved it. Bending over for him, her ass in his face, not being able to see him, letting him have his way with her, doing whatever he wanted to her back there, she loved it. She bore down on the fingers pushing up into her. She opened wider for him and felt really slutty. He circled the fingers around inside her and she rode them, grinding herself down on them, knowing he could see her, that every slutty inch of her was right in his face. She took advantage of that and pushed harder.

"Evie," he begged, "I want to fuck you. Right now. I think you might be ready. Can I try?"

She was beside herself with shock and desire. This was what

she'd been hoping would happen, wasn't it? She swallowed hard. "Okay," she agreed nervously. She expected him to get undressed then, to want her to lie down with him, but he didn't wait for that. He was already trying to mount her from behind. The head of his cock was poised at the opening of her hole.

"You're sure I can do this, Evie? This is what you want?"

"Yes," she told him, not certain, though, of what she was saying. The cock was pressing into her hole now. It was much larger than any fingers. It felt huge. She smothered a quick cry.

"Push yourself on to me," he said. "Open yourself, like you were doing on my fingers."

She did as he asked. She pushed her hole open for him while backing up onto the enormous cock. But it felt very, very different from his fingers. "Oh God," she was crying. "God... oh God!" It felt impossibly huge the thing probing into her. How did other women do this? She was being torn open. But the thought of pleasing him, of giving him what he wanted, kept her pushing, stretching, trying to accommodate him. And Lucas kept steadily easing his thick cock up into her slowly stretching hole.

"I'm almost in," he gasped.

"Jesus, God, Jesus!" she moaned, afraid to move now she felt so thoroughly impaled.

Then he held her hips and began to slowly ease his cock back out.

She whimpered.

He eased the length of his cock back into her, filling her to bursting.

This was nothing like fucking his fingers. She felt stuck there, lodged painfully on his cock, like a pole was shoved up between her legs. Why was she always being such a little fool? What had she been expecting? Anything but this! She was bending over for him like a slut, completely exposed with this enormous thing stuck inside her. And she was absolutely naked while he still had the luxury of wearing most of his clothes. What had happened to being naked together in that motel? "Oh God," she whimpered again as his huge cock pushed back into her, going all the way in now. His balls were pressed right up against her spread and swollen lips. "Oh no," she moaned. "No!" This was too much.

He was picking up speed, finding his rhythm. Holding tight to her ass, he guided his stiff cock in and out, in and out, faster and faster. She was becoming incredibly wet. The thick cock filling her was now slick with her juices.

Suddenly all words escaped her. A new sensation was taking over. Her hole was stretching and stretching, keeping up with the relentless thrusts of his cock. She moaned deliriously in one long grunting, gushing cry. It felt incredible what he was doing to her, and she kept herself poised to take the pounding. She felt filthy like this, but she didn't care. She liked feeling this way. He was fucking her. At long last, he was fucking her. And it seemed like his cock was so swollen it would burst inside her. She pushed herself out even more, her back arched painfully, letting her pussy get really fucked.

Then suddenly, without warning, he pulled out. "Jesus," he cried. "God!"

The warm spurts of his come landed all over her back.

"I'm so sorry," he panted. "Evie, I'm so sorry. I forgot all about condoms. I never thought we would go this far."

And then reality hit her. Her life was going to be very different now. It was scary, what she was capable of doing without even thinking.

Chapter Eleven

In Evie's world, the dam was broken. For once in her life she wished she had a job to go to everyday like normal people did to get her mind off sex. Her lust was heightened now and driving her crazier than ever. It had leaped to a new level. Her lust consumed her. Every moment, day and night, she spent longing for Lucas, longing to feel the thrill of intercourse with him again.

She couldn't leave herself alone. She was wearing herself out touching herself all the time. Even while she slept, she was aware of being lulled in a continual state of arousal. She was always wet, always swollen down there, always on the verge of an orgasm.

It was difficult keeping her world together while she waited for Lucas to call, to tell her the good news that he was taking her to a motel and ecstasy was just around the corner.

A peculiar insanity was overtaking Lucas's world as well. He couldn't remember being this fixated on a woman since he was fourteen-years-old and had walked in on Clarice naked. He thought about Evie incessantly. He found himself with a hard-on in the most inconvenient locations. Too many times now he'd had to excuse himself to the nearest men's room to jerk off. Even then, the relief was fleeting, a temporary condition. Before too long, he'd be fixating on Evie again.

Lucas tried hard to keep a perspective on his work, to fit in his many obligations whenever he wasn't jerking off. He was making himself crazy trying to appear to others as if he were absolutely normal, as if he weren't losing his mind over a woman who was much too young for him. Being anywhere in the vicinity of Big Joe was particularly trying.

He bought a box of condoms and always kept a couple in his pocket and the rest in the glove compartment in his car. He was ready for the next time; he would be prepared. Every morning, he studied his appointments for a break in the endless meetings. He had to get Evie alone again soon or he thought he would lose his mind.

When it became apparent that it would be at least another week before Lucas would have the time to take Evie to a motel, his insanity overtook him. It was very late at night. He was on the river road heading back to New Orleans, the same road where Evie lived. He detoured. He parked his car. He crept up on the Donovan house as quietly as possible. He went around back feeling like a thief in the night, and tossed pebbles at Evie's window.

The clattering rain of pebbles against the glass startled her, but the sight of Lucas Cain down below her window, wearing a suit and tie, was all she needed to see. Still in her summer nightgown, she flew down the backstairs, out into the night and into his arms.

This time they stayed away from the tangled overgrowth of trees. They headed instead to the stretch of secluded lawn behind the ancient gazebo that was in desperate need of repair. There they were free to completely undress and lie down in the grass together, under an impressive canopy of stars.

There was no moon that night. The world was safe and dark. Even on the off chance of someone coming to an upstairs window that late, they weren't likely to be seen.

Lucas didn't even take time to kiss her. He got down between her legs and licked her while she lay flat on her back, holding her thighs open for him, staring up at the stars.

She moaned softly as his expert tongue licked the length of her lips, circled her clitoris, circled her hole. Then a finger slid up inside her, a hint of the ecstasy that was still to come.

Lucas wanted to teach her something new and Evie was all for it.

He straddled her face. She opened her mouth. She knew what he wanted, and she was excited to try it – fellatio.

His thick cock was difficult to accommodate. Her lips were stretched taught around it as Lucas guided it slowly in and out of her mouth. She tried not to gag, but it wasn't easy. The spit collected in her mouth and then trickled down her chin, yet the groans of pleasure that were coming from him now as he slid his cock in and out were irresistible. She let him have his pleasure while she did her best to keep up.

And soon enough they were both on their knees, Lucas behind Evie, a condom securely covering him, and his cock was pushing its way into her, filling her hole. He held her around her belly, keeping her very close. He caressed her tits, tugging at the nipples. He slid his fingers down to her clitoris and rubbed it while they fucked.

Evie came like that almost instantly. The orgasm rocketed

through her. She hadn't expected to feel so excited when he touched her.

He turned her over and asked her to lie down on her back. Then he mounted her that way. He pushed his cock in and she felt herself opening around it, taking it. They fucked like real lovers did, face to face, kissing. Her arms clung to him as the power of his thrusts increased, as he stretched her open, probed down deep in her hole. She was hypnotized by his increasing rhythm. He was coming. He kissed her almost savagely then. His cock pounded into her a few more moments, more slowly, until they were both spent.

***

It was early September. An unexpected heat wave was smothering the Gulf. There was no sign of rain beyond a few quick, fleeting thunderstorms. Afterwards, the humidity was even worse. It hung visibly in the air like a thick haze. The only respite was early morning. From then on the days dragged themselves wetly into the thick evenings.

It was on such a night that Cal Harper was sitting at the Donovan's dinner table, sweating in the air-conditioned room. He was dressed more formally than usual in a suit and tie. He seemed awkward, nervous, a little distracted and preoccupied.

Heat waves sometimes do that to people, Evie thought.

The moment dinner was over Big Joe abruptly excused himself from the table. Evie wouldn't see him again for the rest of the evening, long after Cal Harper had gone home.

Vera helped the cook clear the many dinner dishes from the table, and Cal invited Evie to sit out on the porch swing with him.

"It's awful hot," Evie replied. "Why don't we stay in here?"

"I don't mind the heat, just for a few minutes," he encouraged her. "Come on, Evie. Let's go outside."

With reluctance, she followed him out into the thick air. The sun was sinking in the sky. She sat down beside him on the porch swing.

"Evie," he began, "I'd like to talk about us."

Her stomach clenched. "What us is that?" she asked uneasily.

"Well, you know, you and me… Evie, I'd like to see you more often. I'd like to take you out places, maybe down to have dinner with my folks in the city. I want to spend more time with you."

She stared at him. She didn't have a clue what to say.

"You like me and I like you,' he went on. 'There are things we like to talk about. I don't see why we can't spend more time getting to know each other. Give it some thought," he asked her sincerely. "Please, Evie, I'm getting tired of only being able to see you once a week."

She didn't want to hurt Cal. He was a good man. In fact, she really did like him. But it didn't make any sense to lead him on. She was in love with Lucas Cain. Still, she couldn't find the words that wouldn't hurt Cal, so she just stared at him.

He leaned closer to her, and then kissed her. She hadn't been expecting it. She let him kiss her, though. It was a quick kiss, harmless, or so it seemed. "Shall we go for a ride?" he suggested. "The car's air-conditioned, you know."

"I don't know if I feel like going for a ride tonight, Cal. It's so hot."

"Come on, Evie. You need to get out more. Let's just go take a little drive. Then we'll come back here."

She remembered the last time they'd been alone together in his car. They had kissed. He had felt her up. She remembered how excited it had made her feel. "No," she insisted. "I don't want to go for a drive."

"Well, then let's just take a little walk."

"Cal…"

"Come on, Evie."

She knew what he was up to, he was trying to spend more time with her and make it seem somehow intimate, because he was working up his nerve to ask her to marry him. And Evie knew her father was in on it or he wouldn't have disappeared so early in the evening. "All right," she consented. "But it's so damn hot. I don't want to stay out here for too long."

She followed him out on to the lawn. They walked slowly along the endless flowerbeds while Cal did his best to make small talk. They walked along the path that led to the back lawn. He reached for her hand and held it. She pulled it away. "It's too hot," she tried to explain. "My hands are sweaty."

They walked some more without holding hands. They headed for the shade of a sprawling weeping willow. Once they were under its cover, surrounded by the cascading branches, Cal surprised her by kissing her again. The privacy of the place, the intimacy of it, made him kiss her more passionately then he'd kissed her when they were on the swing.

"Cal, don't." She tried to push him away.

"Evie, honey, I just want to kiss. You like kissing, I know that. I know it's hot out here, but let's kiss." He pulled her to him gently and kissed her mouth again.

She wasn't sure why she was doing it, but she let him kiss her. She opened her mouth for his tongue.

It was no more than a moment before his hand was on her breast, fondling it, finding her nipple through the sheer fabric of her dress.

She moaned. "Cal, no, I don't want to." But her nipple was sensitive. Her body was responding to his touch. "I can't," she insisted. "I don't love you."

"You don't know me," he corrected her. "How can you know if you love me or not? We can enjoy ourselves a little, can't we? We're not hurting anybody by being here like this."

She wanted to leave, but for some reason, she didn't move. Was it because Cal was going to fondle her breast again and she knew it? And then maybe his hand would slide up under her dress, and who knew what else... What was happening to her? Was she so consumed with lust that any man willing to touch her was okay with her? Was this how other girls behaved? Was this what sex was about? "Cal, I can't," she said again.

"All right," he consented. "Then let's just walk."

As he turned away from her, Evie saw the hard-on straining inside his pants he was now in a hurry to conceal.

***

"How was your evening with Cal?" her daddy asked, mysteriously appearing again when she was on her way to her room.

"It was okay," she said. "Cal's nice. He wants me to go into New Orleans with him and have dinner with his parents."

Big Joe was satisfied. "I think that sounds real good, Evie. Why don't you do that?"

She shrugged. "I don't know. I'll think about it."

Alone in her room, she undressed. She wondered about Cal Harper. Who was he really? He was nice, he was rich, educated, he was from a good home, and he clearly had his intentions set on marrying Evie. Still, he couldn't be more different from Lucas Cain if he tried. And yet...

Evie wasn't sure she wanted to think about it, but Lucas

had never once acted like marriage between them was imminent. It was not even hinted at. She wondered now just what his intentions were. She wondered if Lucas had also come from a good home once. Was he rich? Was he educated? She realized that she knew nothing about his background.

She was naked when she slid into bed, and she stroked herself distractedly. She was disappointed. It would have been nice to fool around a little with Cal. Maybe she should have gone ahead and said yes. It's not as though she would have let him get carried away.

She turned over in bed. She felt very confused.

***

Big Joe sat at the breakfast table very early the following morning. He had a day full of meetings ahead but he was in a good humor for a change. "I think Cal Harper's going to surprise Evie. She's going to realize he's a good, reliable fellow, that's what I think."

Vera looked pleased. "When is he going to pop the question?"

"I don't know," Big Joe replied, "but I don't think he's going to wait too long. His father and I are both pressuring him to speed it up. You saw Evie at that party. It's not going to be too long before her dance card is full, and then it'll be hard to control her. She's just like her mother. God knows who she'll wind up with if we leave her on her own."

Vera felt a pang of regret for Evie, but she knew Big Joe was right.

***

Lucas and Big Joe sat down together in the restaurant. They ordered drinks while they waited for the client to show. "I think

I'll cut out early tomorrow," Lucas said. "Make it a half day. I need a little R & R. It's been a while."

Big Joe said, "Sure. I don't see why not. Get a little for me while you're at it. I could use some."

Lucas let the remark slide. It wasn't like him to get too personal with Donovan anyway. But for some reason, Donovan seemed in a talkative mood. In fact, he'd been in a good humor all day.

"You know, Cain," he went on, "in my day, for our R&R, we used to frequent this motel just outside of town. It was pretty sleazy, but it always did the trick. I used to entertain some businessmen from Baton Rouge back then, and this motel had a lounge with the wildest little cocktail waitresses you'd ever want to meet. Of course, I'm talking over twenty years ago. The place is still there, just a lot more run down. Times have changed. I can't imagine the waitresses are anything to shake a stick at anymore. But then I can't imagine you need any help in that department, do you? You've probably got a young one stashed somewhere, don't you, Cain? A real hotty?"

Lucas didn't reply. It seemed like a setup. He concentrated on his drink. Donovan couldn't possibly mean Evie. He couldn't possibly know. If he did, why would he be so cavalier about it and call her a 'hotty'? It would be more likely that he'd smash Lucas right in the jaw. All the same, it made him uneasy. Maybe he was just being paranoid, but maybe he wasn't.

He drank his drink while Donovan rambled on. He played it safe and kept his mouth shut.

Entertaining businessmen from Baton Rouge… Lucas repeated this phrase in his head. Is that what he calls them now, businessmen? Back then they used to be called gamblers, high stakes gamblers. And according to what Miss Willie had always said back on Royal Street, Donovan was bankrolling his long shots against Clarice's inheritance well before they were even married.

"But that was a long time ago," Donovan was saying.

Lucas hadn't heard a word he'd said. He was in his own world again. He'd stopped listening. "Yes it was," he agreed anyway, just to be saying something.

Chapter Twelve

The afternoon when all of Evie's erotic dreams were going to come true the heat wave finally broke. Showers teamed down from the sky.

Lucas had arranged to meet Evie a good distance away from Solisville at a motel that was off the old highway heading up to Baton Rouge. It was a long drive in sheets of steady rain, but Evie didn't mind. She was going to be alone with Lucas finally for an entire afternoon.

The motel was rundown and overgrown. It would have benefited greatly from a lawn mower and a simple coat of white paint, or maybe just a sunny day. Framed by a broken down fence out front was an old swimming pool, decayed and stained with rust. Weeds pushed up through the cracks in the faded blue concrete and drank up the steady downpour. It was a melancholy sight. Evie always thought of swimming pools as a symbol of freedom, of summertime, of school being out and everyone on vacation. Those dream days at this swimming pool were only ghosts now, whoever those days had belonged to.

A cocktail lounge was attached to the motel, but it looked too decadent to hold any charm. Besides, she didn't drink much. And who had time to spend even one minute out in the open amongst people who might just recognize her?

Lucas's black convertible was already in the parking lot.

Evie sat in her car and waited for some sign of him and which room he had taken.

A door opened and there he was, wearing the outfit Evie liked best, a simple white tee shirt and those perfect black trousers. He was barefoot. He looked relaxed.

She got out of her car and darted through the rain. "This place is too much!" she shouted. "How did you ever find it?"

Lucas smiled slyly. "Should I tell you the truth? Your father told me about it at dinner yesterday." He pulled a dripping Evie into the room, and closed the door.

"My father? Why would he know about a place like this?" Then in a corner of her mind she recalled those old postcards she'd found in his drawer during the summer. But those were from a motel that was lively and full of smiling people. "Don't tell me you asked my father to recommend a motel?"

Lucas laughed. "God, no! He had no idea he was being so helpful. He was talking to me about something else."

So this is a motel room, Evie thought. It was a bit of a letdown after all this time. Hotel rooms were a lot nicer. The room was dingy and damp, but at least it was clean. A double bed took up most of the space. Lucas had already pulled back the blankets. She wondered if he was impatient to make love. It excited her to think that he was.

"I think I remember seeing you like this once before," he said.

"What do you mean?"

"I mean drenched. Look at you."

Evie wore a white cotton shirt that was wet and starting to cling, and a pair of blue jeans spattered by raindrops.

Here they were together in broad daylight at last, face to face. She found it a little intimidating to look him in the eye without the night, or at least candlelight, to buffer her. His gaze was challenging, direct, and his brown eyes were so dark they seemed black. And what struck her most was the piercing intelligence she could see in those eyes, as if he were taking in every inch of her and gauging her, somehow.

Even though Cal Harper had graduated from Harvard, she had never seen a spark of life like this in Cal's eyes. "Lucas, where did you go to college?" she asked. It was as good a time as any to get to know him better.

"I didn't," he replied. He sat down on the bed and she sat down next to him.

"You didn't go to college?"

"No. I worked. I've been working since I was ten years old."

"Ten years old? That's crazy."

"Not when you're poor it isn't."

"You were poor?" Evie was shocked. "You mean really poor?" She'd never known anybody who was poor.

"Yes, really poor," Lucas replied. He pulled off his tee shirt and lay back across the bed. Looking up at the stained and peeling ceiling, he added, "I wasn't much different from your father, really. I was born in Bywater, in one of those double shotgun houses just outside the French Quarter. I was illegitimate. I never knew who my father was. I didn't even know my mother for very long. She took off with some guy when I was twelve.

That's when I started working in that call house for room and board, where I knew your parents from. I was very poor back then."

"Lucas, what are you talking about? My father was never poor."

He stared at her. "Of course he was."

"My father? Joseph Donovan? He was never poor."

"Yes, he was, Evie, and he wasn't Joseph Donovan then, he was Joseph Amory. I know, because he came from Bywater."

"Lucas, you're crazy," was all she could think of to say.

He sat up. The look on her pretty face was disturbing. "Maybe I'm wrong, Evie," he acquiesced. "Maybe I'm confusing him with someone else."

He realized now he'd stumbled on to something that he'd never considered, but he should have guessed it that first night when Evie talked about Clarice dying in childbirth. Evie had been raised on the same Donovan myth that had been steadily fed over the years to the entire town of Solisville. She hadn't been told the truth – that her father had married into his fortune and that Clarice DuMaret Donovan had killed herself. She probably didn't even know that Big Joe Donovan might not have been the father of Clarice's baby, of Evie.

"Evie, honey, come here," he said, wanting to protect her. He knew too well how bitter it felt to discover that one's real father might only be a question mark. "Forget about it," he said. "I didn't know what I was saying, and it was a long time ago. I'm sure I was thinking of someone else. Now, don't you want to get out of those wet clothes?"

She was uneasy. "I suppose so." She pulled off her shirt and laid it over the back of a chair to dry. She stepped out of her wet jeans. Why would Lucas make a mistake like that, she wondered.

Why would he get his facts confused no matter how many years ago it was? He worked for her father. He knew him. He saw him everyday. How could he confuse him with someone else?

She undid her bra and stepped out of her panties. Naked, she went over to Lucas, who was waiting for her on the sagging bed. "You weren't mistaken, were you? That story was true. And it was about my father."

"Evie, honey, don't."

He still had his pants on, but now he undressed the rest of the way. He had to get her mind off this or the afternoon would be ruined.

"What did you mean when you said that you worked in a call house, that you knew my parents from there? What's a call house?"

"It's where rich people go to play cards, that's all." He couldn't believe she was this naïve, that she'd been this sheltered. It was like Donovan had raised her in a convent or something. Surely she had to know what prostitutes were?

"A place where rich people go to play cards, like a private club? My parents liked to play cards? And you worked there? Doing what?"

"I helped keep the place clean, ran errands, that kind of thing. Come on, Evie," he said, "this is crazy. Let's not talk about this anymore, let's make love."

She sat down on the bed. Why was it that when it came to her parents, to their lives before she was born, nobody ever wanted to answer her questions?

She had asked Vera who the Donovans were. She had asked her father who the Donovans were.

The reason no one answered her was because there weren't any Donovans. There had never been any Donovans. She would remember the name Amory, though. She would see what kind of an answer she would get from her father now.

Lucas coaxed Evie to lie down next to him. Her body was perfect and now he was finally seeing it in the light. She does look a lot like Clarice, he thought, except maybe for those hairless lips between her legs. He wanted his mouth on her right away. His cock sprang to attention just thinking about it. "Come on, Evie," he tried again. "Relax. We have all afternoon, all evening if you want. We can stay here as long as you'd like." He slipped his hand down between her thighs and nudged them apart. "Wow," he said, trying to cheer her up. "Look at you, you're quite a catch."

Naked, her legs spread wide for her lover's gaze, Evie was starting to remember why they had come to the motel. It was the first time in her life that her pussy had ever been admired. The look on Lucas's face, the obvious lust there as he stared down between her spread legs, made her feel beautiful. She was rapidly forgetting about her father.

Lucas casually stroked his cock while his finger trailed lightly over her smooth lips, and when he ran his finger across the tip of her tender clitoris, her whole body responded, even to that slight touch. She grabbed her thighs and held herself more open, encouraging him to continue exploring. He saw that she was getting wet.

He leaned down and lightly nipped at her clitoris with his lips. A gasp of delight came from her that charged the room. "Do you like this?" he asked, his finger teasing the opening to her hole, his black eyes holding her gaze as he slid his finger in unexpectedly deep.

"Yes," she said, catching her breath. She liked this, she liked being looked at by her lover when he penetrated her.

He watched his finger disappear inside her. Her hole hugged his finger tightly. It was that tightness that tormented him, what he was always thinking of, her tight hole. It was what made him painfully hard whenever he thought of fucking her; it's what set his dreams on fire during the burning nights.

He was getting very aroused now thinking about what his thick cock would look like pushing into that tight hole in broad daylight.

"Lucas," Evie said suddenly, "have you ever been married?"

"No," he replied, sliding his finger in and out, his mind brimming with the possibilities, all the positions he wanted to see her in.

"Do you ever think about it, about getting married?"

"Not really, why?"

Her heart sank a little, but the finger moving in and out of her felt so good. She didn't know why she felt compelled to talk now. She didn't know why she was bringing all this up when all she wanted was to feel this exquisite sensation. His finger was rubbing that spot inside her that felt particularly hard to resist and she moaned. She grasped her thighs tighter, lifting her hole up higher for him, taking his finger in deeper. "My father is trying to marry me off again," she gasped, "to a man named Cal Harper." Her pleasure mounted as the pressure inside her increased. He had slid a second finger into her hole. Together, the fingers fucked her thoroughly, stretched her, rubbed her deep inside. And the look of sheer lust on his face as he watched his fingers fuck her felt almost as good to Evie as the fucking did. "I think Cal's getting ready to ask me to marry him," she sputtered on in spite of herself. "I saw him last night."

"Are you going to tell him yes?" he asked patiently. "Is that what this is about? Are you trying to tell me that it's going to be over between us soon?"

Evie was incredulous. "No!"

"Then why are we talking about this when we should be making love?"

"Because..." her nerve faltered.

He slid his fingers out of her hole and spread himself on top of her.

She wrapped her legs around him. "I love you," she blurted stupidly. "I don't love Cal Harper and I don't want to marry him."

Lucas gazed down into her eyes, his dark hair framing his handsome face. He gently kissed her lips. He said, "If you don't love him then you shouldn't marry him, Evie."

"I know," she said quietly. Why isn't this conversation going anywhere, she wondered. Why won't he say that he loves me? "Lucas?" She tried again.

"What?"

But now he was too close. It was too intimidating. She could feel his warm breath on her face he was that close. When she opened her mouth to speak, he kissed her again, but this time he kissed her passionately, sliding his erection all over her swollen pussy while they kissed. Skin against slippery skin, she moaned deep into his kiss.

"Should we fuck a little bit?" he asked quietly.

She nodded her head.

It took him less than a moment to prepare. When he was ready, she was waiting for him with her knees raised, her thighs spread. She was incredibly wet. He carefully eased his cock into her hole. He laid his weight down on her, and his cock was all the way in.

She cried out as the sheer size of him impaled her, forcing her to stretch open, to let in this intrusion. It felt incredible. She clung to him.

Slowly, Lucas eased his cock in and out, in and out. They had all the time in the world. "Evie," he spoke to her softly while they fucked, "I love you, too, I do, but a marriage between us would be out of the question, you know that."

"No, I don't know that."

They looked into each other's eyes, Evie's pussy stuffed full of his thick cock. He wasn't moving now.

"Honey, there's your father to consider, and my career. Your father would kill me if he even suspected I was seeing you, let alone doing this to you. He'd never allow us to get married. And my career at Donovan & Company would be over. Don't you know that I could move into the top spot there one day?"

"But Lucas, I'm worth a fortune. You wouldn't have to work for my father if we were married."

He pulled out of her abruptly and sat up between her legs. He was angry. "Is that what you think this is about, that I want to marry into your money the way your father did with your mother? I idolized him, Evie, that much I admit, but only because I loathed being poor, not because I wanted to get married to an inheritance like he did. I just wanted to make a success of my life. And I have."

She was stunned. Was he saying that his career was more important than loving her? That her father had used her mother for her money? "Lucas, that's mean," she cried, "all of it! You're mean!"

"I don't want to be mean, Evie. I love you, but my career is very important. I've worked for this my whole life. You and I have only known each other a few short months. How can you possibly know that you want to be married to me? You don't know me."

To Evie's complete humiliation, she began to cry. "I don't

understand you at all, Lucas, you know that? I don't understand how you feel, I don't understand whatever it is you keep trying to insinuate about my parents; I don't understand anything."

"Evie, my God, don't cry, we're supposed to be enjoying ourselves. We've been looking forward to this. Why spoil it now?"

"I'm sorry if I'm spoiling everything, but I just don't understand you!"

Lucas got off the bed in a huff and went and sat in a chair. "You're exasperating, Evie, you know that? What is it that you want from me?"

I want to get married! she felt like shrieking. Instead, she glared at him through her tears. "I don't want anything from you," she said. "Nothing."

He tried frantically to figure out why it was all falling to pieces. "Jesus, Evie," he said, "I love you. Isn't that enough for now? Can't we just enjoy what we're doing now and let the rest of life take care of itself? I want to make love to you very much, that hasn't changed. What is it about that that's so hard to understand?"

"Nothing," she was forced to admit. She, too, wanted very much to make love. What would it matter if they didn't talk about getting married right now? Right now, they could at least make love.

She stopped crying.

"Come here," he said.

Reluctantly, she got up off the bed.

"Closer," he said. "Come right over here. Kiss me."

She leaned down and kissed him, slipping her tongue into his mouth, her pretty brown hair falling into his face.

He caressed her tits while they kissed, tugging on her nipples insistently. He had won her again. He had her complete attention. He took her face in his hands. "I want you to bend over for me," he said. "I want to fuck you that way, okay?"

She smiled very sweetly. "Okay," she said.

Chapter Thirteen

It was very late when Evie finally forced herself to leave the motel. She still had a long drive home, but at least the rain had stopped and the night was clear.

Lucas walked her to her car. He leaned down and kissed her again through the open car window as she sat in the front seat and tried to make herself stick her key into the ignition. She could smell herself on Lucas's lips while they kissed. It aroused her again. She wanted to get out of the car and start all over. He was spending the night in the motel room and heading into Solisville in the morning. She wanted to stay right there with him and fuck him all night, but she knew it was too risky.

"Goodnight," they finally said.

She pulled her car out of the parking lot and onto the highway, heading for home.

Lucas headed back to the room. He smelled her musky scent

on his fingers. He got another erection. He was going to jerk off before getting into the shower. It was going to be a long night.

***

On the long drive home, Evie felt elated. She was truly in love. She knew she was going to marry Lucas Cain. It was going to happen. She was too much in love to believe otherwise. Cal Harper was just a speck of dust on the face of a distant planet.

She squirmed restlessly in the car seat, getting wet again, and her tender nipples ached. She'd stuffed her bra into her purse, not wanting to be bothered with it, and now her swollen nipples rubbed against her cotton shirt. Lucas had practically chewed on them.

When would they get another chance to go back to that crazy motel? She was eager to fuck him again. She wanted her pussy all over his face; she wanted to feel his cock filling her; she wanted to bend over for him; she wanted to feel the power of his cock sliding in and out of her mouth…

She had to stop this. She was getting too horny. She had to keep driving. Her father was going to be livid as it was. She was so late, and she hadn't bothered to call anyone to at least let them know she was okay.

She was rebelling all the way now, and she didn't care. It didn't matter to her if anybody was worried. She was chipping away her father's hold on her. She was living her own life.

When she pulled her car into the driveway, all the lights on the first floor were on. Before she was even out of the car, her father was standing on the veranda. When she came up the porch steps, he said, "Where've you been? Was tonight your dinner in New Orleans with Cal's parents?"

"No," she said. "I wasn't in New Orleans and I wasn't with Cal."

"Well, where were you?"

Evie knew that with Cal Harper no longer the topic of this conversation, her father was not going to stay patient for very long. "Why does it matter where I was? I'm home now."

"What kind of an answer is that?"

"It's not much of an answer," she agreed quietly, trying to keep her nerve, "but I have a question for you."

Her boldness caught Big Joe off guard. "What is it?" he asked.

"Who were the Amorys, the ones from Bywater?"

Big Joe looked like he was going to succumb to a heart attack right there on the porch and Evie immediately regretted the callousness of her question. Nevertheless, she was angry and she wanted her question answered. From the look on her father's face and the lack of his ready denial, she knew the things Lucas had told her were true. "Did you marry my mother for her inheritance?" she pressed on.

"Evie!" Vera shouted. She'd been listening at the screen door and now she stormed out onto the porch in her bathrobe and slippers. "How can you say a thing like that to your father?"

"It's all right," Big Joe said calmly. "I'll handle this, Vera, go back inside, please. Evie," he began slowly, "I don't know where you've been tonight, who you've been with or what they've been telling you, but I loved your mother. I married your mother because I loved her."

"That's not what I heard," she blurted. "I heard that you were poor and that you married her to get rich."

Big Joe wanted to slap her face, but he didn't. "Do you know how ugly you sound? You don't have a clue what you're even talking about."

"I heard it from somebody who came from Bywater, who knew you as Joseph Amory. He knew you and my mother a long time ago. He knew what he was talking about. You can't lie to me anymore!"

"I may have been poor, Evie, I may have even changed my name. Maybe I didn't like the people I came from, but none of that means I didn't love your mother."

She stood there and stared at him, anger shooting out of her eyes. "Why did you have to tell me lies, daddy? Why couldn't you have just told me the truth? What else have you told me that was just lies?" She was in tears now. "You never want to talk about my mother. I know next to nothing about her. I never knew she'd even owned a simple thing like a bible until a couple months ago. I never knew you'd spent your honeymoon in a cheap motel. And why was that, anyway, because you were footing the bill and not her? I only found out tonight that she liked to play cards, a simple thing like that!"

"What are you talking about now? Your mother never liked to play cards." Big Joe was bewildered. "What makes you think she liked to play cards?"

"I know all about that call house, where you used to play cards."

So it had finally happened, Big Joe realized, the axe he feared had fallen. She'd somehow managed to wind up in the vicinity of Lucas Cain. That's what this was about. How much had he told her? How much damage was done? "Evie, I want you to go to your room now. I'm through talking for tonight. I've had it with you."

"You've had it with me?" she cried incredulously.

"Yes," he shouted, "I've had it with you. We can talk about this some other time, when you haven't had me up all night worrying about you because you wanted to go carousing 'til all hours with Lucas Cain!"

Evie was stopped cold. How could he know about that? And how much did he know? Had someone been spying on them while they'd been having sex? She was mortified. She felt completely exposed.

Big Joe could tell by his daughter's stunned face that he'd hit the nail on the head. He felt sick; he felt enraged. "Where did you wind up meeting?" he badgered her.

"Nowhere," she insisted. "I wasn't anywhere with Lucas Cain."

"Just tell me, Evie. I'm going to find out anyway, even if I have to rip his tongue out to get the answer, I'll find out."

His anger was so severe that she felt she had to say something. "We met a good ways from here," she said vaguely, "toward Baton Rouge."

Big Joe looked mystified. "Baton Rouge?" But then the pieces fell together quickly. "Baton Rouge?" he shouted. "You mean he took you to that motel? You were in a motel with Lucas Cain?" He grabbed her roughly by the arm. "Please tell me you were in the lounge, Evie. Please tell me that's where he took you, to have drinks in the lounge."

She swallowed hard. He was hurting her arm and pulling her too close to his rage, right up into it. And she understood now, she understood thoroughly why Lucas hadn't wanted her father to find out. This rage of his was going to go somewhere, but she was afraid to think where. "Yes," she tried agreeing meekly, "we just had some drinks."

Big Joe stared her down, not believing a word of it. "And that's why you couldn't manage to crawl in until almost two in the morning, because you'd had a couple drinks? In a motel that's clear out of town? Where no one would see what you were doing?" Just as roughly, he let go of her arm, as if he were trying to throw her away. "You're just like your mother, you know that?" he said savagely. "There's just no saving girls like you."

Vera was crying now. Through the screen door, her sobs could be plainly heard on the porch. It sobered Big Joe enough to tell Evie, in a more rational manner, to go to her room.

"But I'm almost twenty-two," she shrieked, clearly pressing her luck with him. "I'm tired of being told what to do! I'm tired of being told to go to my room!"

Big Joe suddenly looked exhausted. "Trust me," he assured her, "I know how old you are. I was there when you were born. I remember it well. And I remember what it's been like, every single day of the nearly twenty-two years of your life, to raise you by myself because your mother is dead. I just want you to go to your room now, that's all. I don't care if you're ninety-two. Just go to your room. It's two o'clock in the morning. We're all going to go to our rooms."

***

Big Joe retired to the master suite. It was all so grand. The suite fairly crackled with history. Such a long line of savvy DuMarets had done the best they could to survive their own lives inside these walls, year after year after year, until two centuries had passed and not a single one of them had figured out how to outlive life. Every last one of them was dead. And now it all belonged to a couple of Donovans, to Evie and him. They owned it all.

Well, to an Amory and one last DuMaret.

But Big Joe wasn't about to give in to that, not because of some upstart like Lucas Cain. He stopped himself from feeling so defeated. He was a Donovan, no matter what had been said about his mother back in Bywater. And Evie was a Donovan, too, because he himself had raised her. It was his name on her birth certificate and, who knew for sure? Maybe he really was Evie's father. Maybe he had fathered her that night. Maybe he had. Besides, it didn't matter because Clarice had wanted him to be the father, had hoped he was the father, and Big Joe had married Clarice and had raised Evie to be his own.

Big Joe went over to the bar and poured himself a stiff drink. He needed more than cognac now. He needed something hard-hitting like bourbon, something not quite so refined.

What was he going to do about Cain besides kill him?

There wasn't an easy answer. Cain had become instrumental to him in a very short time. He'd fallen into the job so seamlessly. And it was Cain's charm that had helped Big Joe win over a lot of clients. Cain was an expert at charming clients' wives. But now Big Joe wanted to spit when he thought of Cain trying out that kind of charm on Evie.

What more did Cain want, anyway? Wasn't he grooming Cain to take over the company one day? Did he have to own every-thing, including Evie?

Big Joe had plans for his daughter, plans that he'd crafted carefully for over twenty years. And those plans included giving Evie a rich and stable life, something a serious, if maybe a bit col-orless, man like Cal Harper could give her. A man like Lucas Cain had nothing to offer her, no background, no education, no heritage. He was a bastard from the street.

And it was a bastard from the street – he himself, Joseph Amory – who had been Clarice's undoing. He wasn't going to let history repeat itself with Evie.

Big Joe downed his drink. He switched off the light in the study and retired to his bedroom. It was sickening. How many times would he have to look at that old bed before he no longer saw the ghost of Clarice, her lifeless body lying there, her suicide note placed just so on his pillow? How would he ever forget a sight like that? How could he ever eradicate that overwhelming feeling of grief and loss? It receded, but it never fully went away. And how would he ever undo his guilt? He had let her down without even knowing it was happening. His eyes had been too full of ignorant greed to see anything else.

It was always on nights like this that her ghost returned with a vengeance; nights when he felt particularly weak and defeated. The bourbon coursed through his veins now, but it wouldn't help Big Joe sleep, he already knew that. He'd get into bed, and whether or not the lights were out, the pictures would start. The movie of his life, unexpurgated, all the obscenities that had been his early ambitions, still there in living color.

Reel one was himself as a young man, uneducated, the illegitimate son of an immigrant housemaid, Beatrice Amory, and a wealthy lawyer, Donald Donovan. The scenes from his impoverished childhood in Bywater weren't quite as colorful as the later scenes of his life, his marriage to an heiress, yet they were oddly more pleasant. Beatrice Amory, though essentially penniless and disgraced by the reprehensible Donald Donovan, had been a good mother. But she'd neglected to send little Joseph to Sunday school, to familiarize him with that all-important commandment about not coveting what belongs to thy neighbor. Joseph had grown into the living embodiment of avarice, that mighty sin of greed.

In reel two he lives alone in a room in the Vieux Carré and spies Clarice DuMaret coming out of Antoine's very late one night. He knows full well who she is because he's made an art of memorizing who's worth how much in New Orleans. Miss DuMaret stands to inherit a hefty fortune, well into the multimillions, at least in the value of her real estate. However, he hasn't expected Clarice to sprout into a young woman of such joie de vivre. It's genuine, his plea to her that night to allow him to treat her to an after dinner drink somewhere. It's also genuine, his joy when she accepts. Reel two is always the shortest reel. It's the only time in his life he can remember being guileless.

Without fail, reel three consumes most of the wee hours of the morning. It's the reel where hedonism has the starring role. Joseph takes full advantage of Clarice's loose purse strings to introduce her to the pricier vices like opium and cocaine, expensive champagnes and high stakes poker. Well, the high stakes poker was never a vice she took to, so Joseph himself imbibed while Clarice went off in search of other temptations.

In reel three, sexual lasciviousness vies with hedonism for top billing. Joseph deflowers Clarice solely because it gets her, finally, into those lewd positions he more readily favors over sexual abstinence. In no time at all, her fondness for cocaine and champagne gives her one raging, insatiable libido. Night and day, Clarice is in the sack with someone, mostly Joseph, and sometimes Joseph along with an interested third party, but sometimes it's someone entirely new who Joseph never encounters. He's too busy gambling her money away in poker games with high rollers from Baton Rouge.

When they marry, it's because she's knocked-up or 'pregnant' as the discreet doctor informs them. They were practically engaged anyway, since Joseph was always pledging his undying affection to her. They have a hasty marriage at City Hall followed by a wild romp in a sleazy motel – Clarice's idea, since Joseph always favored the five-star establishments she could easily afford. But on her one and only wedding night, Clarice opted to go slumming, and the wedding night was bliss. Clarice was so trashed that Joseph had her in his favorite position, uninterrupted, all night long.

Reel four flies by quickly. It's where Clarice introduces her new husband, the fortune-hunting Joseph, to her father, an actual DuMaret descended from a long, rich line of DuMarets. Her father is not amused by this development. In fact, it gives the old geezer a fatal heart attack, and Joseph couldn't be more pleased. His late father-in-law's wedding gift to him? Clarice has abruptly come into her full inheritance. As the human incarnate of greed, how could Joseph have asked for anything more?

Reel five is a killer though. It's where Clarice discovers that Joseph loves her money more than he loves her, and that it's pretty much always been that way. Her emotions already extreme because of her pregnancy, she lapsed into a severe depression. She blames herself for her father's untimely death. She blames herself for the accidental pregnancy. She blames herself for the empty marriage. And in her even more severe post-partum depression, she takes her own life, leaving everything but the house and land in a trust fund to her baby, Evie, ensuring that Joseph can't fritter away her daughter's fortune, but that he can at least try to keep a good, solid roof over her tiny head.

The denouement is Joseph alone and grieving, faced with the hideousness of his errors and a baby to feed. Too late for Clarice, he is baptized by the fire of his self-revulsion and is re-born. And as is so often the case with converts his conversion is severe. He vows to shelter little Evie from greedy men like him no matter what it takes, for Clarice's sake, and perhaps to assuage his searing conscience.

Chapter Fourteen

Lucas didn't get much sleep. His eyes opened at the first light of dawn poking in through the battered window shade, his body aching from the sagging mattress and the damp air in the motel room. What little sleep he'd gotten during the night had been fitful. His dreams had been rife with a sense of foreboding, and images of making love to Evie kept blurring into his memories of Clarice.

He lay in bed now in a half-sleep, piecing together what he could of his dreams. He realized he hadn't thought about Clarice in months, not since he'd first started working for Donovan. For a man who had been haunted by a woman for so many untold years, it was curious to Lucas that he hadn't even noticed when the images of Clarice had left for good. He knew it was because of Evie. She was his dream girl now. She was more than that, because she was the real thing, flesh and blood. And he loved her.

He loved her in a way that he had never loved Clarice. Fantasies became obsolete when real love became tangible in a man's world.

Real love? He stared up at the ceiling. How could he even be considering it? In too many ways, Evie was like a little girl. What was he supposed to do, wait twenty years until she could crawl out from under Donovan's fantastic shadow, the mythical world he kept her locked in? It's no wonder Donovan wanted to keep everyone clear of his daughter, especially anyone who might have spent any time in the Quarter too many years ago. Donovan's precarious house of cards could easily come tumbling down.

And he had gone to such lengths to build it! Lucas was putting it all together now. A private boarding school up north to ensure Evie's childhood was spent away from home. And what did her home consist of when she was there? An antebellum mansion far removed from the common experience of anyone else in town. Who could she relate to in a town that, by then, had been spoon fed the same myths about her beginnings as she had, until a new reality had emerged to supplant the old one? Donovan was safe as long as he could control the ways Evie interacted with the outside world, arranging dates that would lead, with luck, to an arranged marriage, a veritable financial merger, a new and improved Donovan empire.

What would have been so terrible, Lucas wondered, if Evie had been told the truth from the beginning, that her father had changed his name and that he'd once been poor? Or that her mother had been beautiful but tragic? It would have helped Evie grow up, and it certainly would have saved Lucas from a few awkward moments.

Lucas dragged himself out of bed. The room was so damp and

cloying he needed yet another shower before making the long drive into work. He switched on the bathroom light, one dim naked bulb jutting out grimly from what was once a pair of sconces on the bathroom wall. The bathroom sink and toilet were stained with rust, and the shower stall was lined with crumbling, broken tiles. The flimsiest shower curtain in the world hung on rusted rings and clung uncomfortably to his long legs when he turned on the shower.

He stood under a trickle of tepid water and tried to imagine a motel like this ever having held any conceivable charm. But then, he figured, cocktails and cocktail waitresses could go a long way towards lending charm to any establishment. I'm sure men like Donovan took plenty of turns with those cocktail waitresses in these very beds, he thought, back in its heyday. Either way, though, the motel was long past its prime now.

He shut off the water. For a quick moment, he tried to picture what Donovan's reaction would be if he ever got wind of what Lucas had been doing with Evie in one of these same rundown beds. He knew a thing like that would get ugly and there was no way his job would survive it. He was going to have to be very, very careful about seeing Evie. How could she even be thinking about getting married? He asked himself that as he fixed his hair in the mirror. It's as if she didn't know her own father.

He dressed and left the room, then got into his convertible. For the first time in ages, he took the top down. He was going to enjoy the drive into Solisville. It was a beautiful blue morning.

***

Lucas arrived early at the Solisville office and Thomas, Big Joe's driver, was already planted in the parking lot, the black Lincoln, as always, brightly gleaming in the sunshine.

It wasn't unusual for Donovan to be at the office so early; he lived for his empire. What was unusual, however, was Donovan's disheveled appearance. He looked to Lucas as if he hadn't slept a wink. His stomach churned. This was probably because Evie had gotten home so late. The poor bastard hadn't slept.

"Cain," Donovan snapped, "I want to speak to you in my office, now."

"Let me just grab a cup of coffee–"

"No, right now, Cain."

Damn, Lucas thought, it was hitting the fan already. This has to have something to do with Evie…He had to think fast. What would be his defense?

"How was your R&R, Cain?" Donovan asked suspiciously, motioning to Lucas to take a seat. "Did you make good use of your time off?"

"Yes," Lucas replied evenly, "I did."

"Good." Big Joe sat down behind his desk. He said nothing for a moment. Then without warning he heaved a solid glass paperweight through the air, cracking it against the far wall of the office and denting the wall.

Lucas made a heroic effort to remain unfazed.

"The only reason your head didn't get in the way of that, Cain," Big Joe shouted, "is because I've got better things to do with my life than go to prison for killing a piece of garbage like you! Tell me something," he went on, "what kind of thrill do you get from chopping me down at the knees? How does it feel to cash my checks one minute and then go screw my daughter the next? Is it something you can explain to me?"

"I don't screw your daughter," Lucas replied calmly, knowing there was no point in lying? "I'm in love with your daughter. There's a big difference."

"I'm not going to argue semantics with you. I told you from day one to keep away from her, Cain! How could you do this to me? And in a motel room, of all the cheap and disgusting places!" Big Joe sank back in his chair, remembering all those nights Evie had snuck out of the house. He realized now that there might be other men, other motel rooms, other even seedier places. This was, after all, Clarice's daughter they were talking about. My daughter, he reminded himself, my daughter.

"Why does this have to be about you anyway?" Lucas asked, getting angry now watching his career go down the drain, and feeling he had nothing to lose by going for broke. "Why can't this be about Evie and I being in love?"

"Because I have plans for Evie, important plans. I want her to have a good solid future. And if I left it up to her, she'd marry a big fat question mark like you, a man who takes her to only the finest places, apparently. If I left things up to Evie, Cain, she would choose a man like you. She did choose a man like you."

"Nobody chose anybody, it just happened. We're in love."

Big Joe was outraged. "But she's marrying Cal Harper!"

"I think that's up to her!"

"She's not marrying you, Cain."

"Who said anything about Evie marrying me?"

This caught Big Joe by complete surprise. Weren't they talking about Evie's fortune here? He stared Lucas down, not sure whether to slug him for not even offering to do right by his daughter, or to feel relieved that perhaps there was a loophole here, something he hadn't counted on. There was no marriage underway, only a brief affair... "Cain," he said, measuring his words carefully, "you've been very useful here, more than useful, an asset. Until now, you've worked out very well. We're businessmen, right? Why can't we agree to separate business from pleasure once and for all?"

"What are you talking about?" Big Joe sounded as if he were negotiating.

"I mean cut me some slack, Cain. Keep away from Evie. Let her get over you. I want her to marry Cal Harper. I need some room to maneuver here. You do this for me, and I don't see why we can't go on just like before."

Lucas was stunned. He'd expected to be fired. He'd never expected a proposition on Evie's happiness. "You want me to act like it never happened; to stop loving her, just like that?"

"Cain, have you ever heard of loving from afar? Haven't you ever known a woman who was too beautiful to touch? A woman who really got to you, but you could only screw in your head?"

"You mean like your wife?" he offered darkly. "You want to add your daughter to that lofty company? You're a peach, Donovan."

Big Joe wanted to slug him for that remark, but he pushed his vitriol aside. This was business now. He lit a cigarette to buy himself some time. He needed this agreement from Cain – that he would stop seeing Evie. He couldn't let things get too ugly, to the point of no return. "Can't we keep my wife out of this?" he asked. "Can we try to be a little civilized here? I'm asking you to do this favor for Evie, Cain, for her future, her long-term happiness, as opposed to some cheap thrill in a motel room that's going to burn itself out."

This was a point Lucas hadn't considered yet, that this was an affair that might burn itself out.

"At least think about it, Cain. Do me that favor. Take another day off if you have to and give it some thought. We can be reasonable, right? We're talking long-term, remember?" Big Joe repeated the phrase "long-term" for emphasis because he saw the effect it was having on Lucas. His wheels were turning. They might just get out of the woods yet.

***

Lucas got in his convertible and got the hell out of Solisville. He took the highway into New Orleans and avoided the river road entirely. He didn't want to run the risk of so much as glimpsing Evie. He needed to think.

When he reached his house in the Lower Garden District, an angry cloud of gloom was seeping into him. His chest was tight. Lucas felt like he could barely breathe, and it wasn't the humidity. It was the thoughts that were in his head.

Evie was young, too young yet to know what it meant to come from a good family line, what the value of that could be. Whoever this Cal Harper was, it was a safe bet that Donovan had had him checked thoroughly, from past to present. When the lust of the moment between himself and Evie had played out, where was Evie going to get the kind of future a woman like her deserved? If they continued to see each other, Lucas would be out of a job. He'd be back in the Quarter scrambling for another trip up the ladder. He had no past, no heritage, no family influence in business affairs to help smooth things over. He made good money, but he was hardly what anyone would call rich. If he did one day take over Donovan & Company it would happen far in the future. Of course, that could only happen if he stayed away from Evie.

Was there any alternative? He could continue seeing her in spite of her father's objections, lose his job and then live off Evie's money until she grew tired of the arrangement and moved on.

Everywhere Lucas's dejected mind turned, it looked as if there was no other way that made sense. The best way, it seemed, was the only solution that looked after everyone's interests. Lucas would leave Evie alone, keep his job, keep Donovan happy, and give Evie a shot at a future that was more suited to an heiress.

He searched his kitchen for something to alleviate his distress. The last thing he wanted to do now was jerk-off. Instead, he did the next best thing. He wrapped his fist around the neck of a cold bottle of beer, and kept them coming for the rest of the morning.

***

Big Joe was out of the office again before nine o'clock a.m., one of his shortest days on record. He tried to pull himself together in the back seat of the Lincoln. This business with Cain looked like it was going to clear. He was going to go home and force Evie to have lunch with Cal Harper today. Something very civilized, that both he and Cal's father would attend. It would be three against Evie, and they were going to win.

Chapter Fifteen

That morning, Evie slept late. When her eyes opened, it was already nine o'clock. She was tucked inside the antique mahogany four-poster, safe behind the mosquito netting, in the bed that had mocked her all summer and had now become her sanctuary. She was hiding from the world and she was in no hurry to get out of bed.

She was sure her father would have left for the office early; that he was long gone. He wouldn't want to miss a moment of confronting Lucas if he could, she knew that. But there was still Vera lurking about, and she wasn't in the mood to confront her, either.

She hadn't slept much during the night. Around dawn she had tried to leave word for Lucas at the front desk of the motel, warning him not to go to work, to go home and buy them some time. But she had no way of knowing if Lucas had gotten her message or not. The night clerk hadn't sounded as if he understood much English. If she was going to hear anything upsetting from Lucas, it was probably going to be around now. And so far, the phone hadn't rung.

During what little time she had slept, Evie's dreams had been fitful. Mostly she dreamed of Lucas, but he would blur into vague images of her father, only he wasn't her father, it was a man named Joseph Amory. He was understood to be Evie's father, but he looked just like Lucas. In her dream, it was hard to tell them apart, these two Lucas Cains, which made the sex parts of the dream incredibly difficult. If Evie wasn't careful, she would find herself making love to a Lucas who was really Joseph Amory. A few times she slipped up and caught herself making love to her own father, but the scene would abruptly change. Evie would turn into her mother, and then she'd be watching her own parents have sex.

Dream after dream after dream had gone just like that. It was maddening, and each time she would awaken with a start, fearing her father, feeling his overwhelming presence coming from the room just down the hall. She was afraid of what he was going to do when the sun finally came up.

Yet part of her was still stuck in a swoon from all those hours she'd spent at the motel making love with Lucas. It was the feeling that always wound up garnering most of Evie's attention, her lust for Lucas. It was stronger than any fear of her father. It knew no bounds. How many times had she lain there during the night with her fingers once again between her legs? It became like an irresistible tape loop. Images from the motel, of what their bodies had done together, pulled at her memory and she'd come again and again and again. Even now, while her nervous stomach churned over the unknown fate awaiting her and Lucas, she was yet again thinking about that motel.

What had delighted her most had been the unfamiliar feeling that they'd had nothing but time ahead of them. They'd made love without worrying, without rushing, without fearing they were going to get discovered. It had heightened the lovemaking, allowing each sensation to linger and build. It had allowed the sexual exchanges between them to become truly intimate. A physical trust had grown between them it had never occurred to Evie could exist between two people.

But that's what it means to be lovers, she realized now, that trust, that willingness to be vulnerable and explore each other's bodies together.

"I like it best when you're on top like this," Lucas had said. "I can have my arms full of you, and I can get my cock up inside you all the way. It feels incredible."

It was the first time Evie had ever been on top. She noticed right away that this position opened her hole right up so his cock could get all the way in. She could sit down on it until his cock was so far up inside her she ached. She liked being able to look down at him while they were fucking. She liked watching his hands on her tits, pulling on her nipples, as she rubbed her whole mound around on him, feeling her vagina opening somewhere clear up inside her as it got probed and probed and probed...

She was horny again. This was getting ridiculous. At some point she was going to have to get out of bed. But for now she was at herself again, her fingertips rubbing rapidly against her already engorged clitoris. She tugged at one of her nipples. At first it was too sore, but it gave itself over to the persistent tugging. Soon enough, tiny waves of intense pleasure were building in her stiff nipple as she pestered it. She tugged at the other nipple until it, too, was delivering a shooting twinge of pleasure. She kept it up with each tit, wishing for a third hand, better yet wishing for Lucas's mouth, for his expert tongue. It would be good to feel it right now on one of her aching nipples... or to have his mouth down there between her legs, right on her swelling clit, where her fingers were not letting up on their pressure.

The day before she had lost track of how many hours she'd spent with Lucas's face between her legs. He seemed to love licking her, sucking on her, and then mercilessly tormenting her sensitive clit. She liked that she had no hair down there now, that she could see everything.

Once, Lucas made her stand and look down at herself, at how her clitoris was so stiff and erect it was puffing out noticeably from between her sex lips. She'd never seen her clitoris looking so swelled up before.

"Do you think you could come like this?" he'd asked, down on his knees in front of her. "With me licking lightly on just this little tip?"

Evie didn't reply, she gasped. That little tip was incredibly engorged and responsive. True to his word, Lucas did nothing but lick at it lightly, no fingers, no pulling aside of the lips. Just his tongue licking lightly across this exposed nub that she could plainly see protruding out from her mound with her own eyes. It hadn't taken long for her to come like that. She had also come bending clear over for him, grabbing her ankles.

"Hold on," he'd said. "See if you can do it!"

They were both giggling she looked so contorted, but when his mouth went down underneath her, when it honed in on her clitoris, hanging stiff, the lips parting to expose it, she wasn't giggling, she was coming. "Oh God!" She couldn't keep from grunting, from crying out. She'd never come that fast. She held tight to her ankles and thrust herself open, letting her unprotected clit get sucked hard. His face was stuffed right up in there, until the force of her climax had her whole mound riding his merciless tongue.

Evie was ready to come again now just thinking about it. So many salacious pictures were filling her head, too many to keep up with in fact, because the endless images of him fucking her were just now beginning to surface.

She moaned urgently in her bed, keeping the intensity of the orgasm to herself, rubbing her clitoris like mad as a flood of lusty memories shoved past her mind with the force of a tidal wave.

She came as quietly as she could, but the climax had exhausted her.

She made a gallant effort to get out of bed. It wasn't easy, but she at least made it to the bathroom. Whether or not she'd simply go back to bed afterwards was something she'd decide later.

In the shower, fragments of her dream of the two Lucas Cains came back to her, and it occurred to her now that Lucas Cain and her father were in fact very similar. Not just that they came from these strange beginnings in Bywater, but more in the way they looked, dark and tall. Physically, her father and Lucas looked a lot alike.

Now suddenly, for the first time, Evie could see her father from her mother's point of view. Her parents, she realized, were a lot like she and Lucas. Her mother had been significantly younger than her father, and her mother had been the one with more money. Her mother had fallen for a dark-haired man from Bywater. There were so many similarities it was like history repeating itself.

She thought about her parents spending their honeymoon in the Hi Life Motel. It had probably been a place similar to the motel she and Lucas had gone to, and now she saw her parents' honeymoon in a whole new light. It didn't matter what a room looked like, if it was cheap or expensive, what counted were the people in the room.

Evie smiled to herself. She believed now that her parents really had been in love, that they'd done crazy things. It made her happy to think that maybe her parents had once done it at the same motel she'd been in. After all, it was her father who had told Lucas about the place. Maybe they'd been there when they were just lovers in love.

She was going to have to figure out a way to be nicer to her father, she thought, even though she knew he was really angry right now. It was only temporary. Somewhere down underneath it all, there was a man who had been in love once, too, in love with a woman who had died too young. It hadn't been just about her mother's money.

Her father would have to see that Lucas was facing the same thing now, being in love with a woman who was worth a fortune, a woman whose bank account could easily hurt his pride. And her father was only making it worse with this silly rule about keeping his business associates separate from his family; creating some sort of class war.

Evie regretted that Cal Harper didn't work for Donovan & Company. It would give her a ready excuse to turn down any of his proposals.

Finally, she got dressed. She'd made up her mind that she was going to embrace this day, whatever was coming.

On her way downstairs, something struck her. Another good thing was going to come from this news about her father's past, his poverty; this family named Amory. Now there would be no more reason for him to be so secretive. Now maybe he would feel more comfortable talking to Evie. And now maybe everyone could just relax about Evie's mother.

***

The gleaming black Lincoln pulled up the drive to the house, and Big Joe got out. "Wait here," he told Thomas. "We're having lunch in the city today. We'll be leaving soon." He went inside and was pleased to find Evie talking with Vera in the kitchen, looking fresh and pretty. "Did you sleep well?" he asked.

Vera cut in, "I hope so. She's just now getting out of bed."

"I didn't sleep great," Evie said. "But it was okay."

"Well you look great." Big Joe lamented what he was getting ready to do her, but he'd come up with a plan that he thought would at least get Evie into the car. "We're going into New Orleans today," he said. "Right now, in fact. We're going to have lunch out." As he had hoped, Evie misinterpreted this to mean the two of them were having lunch together, alone, not with others, least of all with the Harpers. "You look really pretty," he added. "Maybe you were reading my mind. Did you suspect you were going to have a lunch date today?"

"No," she answered. She was relieved that her father was in such good spirits, that the shouting seemed to be over. Maybe the problem with Lucas was gone for good. She had the distinct impression that her father had seen Lucas and that they'd already talked about things. It seems to have gone well, she decided. He looks very, I don't know, almost serene. Maybe this means Lucas will be keeping his job. Maybe this is what lunch is about, maybe it's about a peace offering regarding Lucas and me.

***

The back of the Lincoln was dark and cool. Evie couldn't remember the last time she'd ridden in the back of this ostentatious car with her father, or the last time Thomas had driven her anywhere. She started to see how, over the last few months, she had managed, finally, to become more independent. She was doing things her own way. It wouldn't be much longer, she decided, before she got up her nerve to move out of the old DuMaret mansion altogether and find a place of her own.

The mood in the car between Evie and her father was stiff, at best. She was on edge waiting for him to bring up the topic of Lucas Cain, or to rehash what had happened the night before, to bring up the Amorys, to bring up anything about Bywater. But he said nothing along those lines. Instead, Big Joe made awkward stabs at small talk that put her even less at ease.

"When was the last time you had lunch in New Orleans?" he asked.

Evie couldn't remember.

"That old French Quarter has a lot of history, doesn't it? I don't suppose you've ever really spent much time there."

"No daddy, none at all, really."

"Have you ever given any thought to living closer to the city? Leaving Solisville maybe?"

"I suppose so."

"You have?" Big Joe was fishing for any signs, any clues at all, to indicate that Evie had been to Lucas Cain's house, that she might know where he lived and might want to live closer to him, or that they'd spent any time together in the Quarter where she might have been recognized by someone who'd known her mother. I'm getting too paranoid, he told himself. I need to knock this off. Things are going to go just fine. "I'm surprised to hear you say that, Evie. You always struck me as wanting to stick around Solisville. Where around the city have you thought you might like to live?"

"Well, I haven't really thought about it that far."

"Would you like something cold to drink?"

"No, thank you."

"I don't suppose you had much of a chance to eat breakfast. Seems like you slept awful late."

She shrugged and left it at that.

"We're having lunch at a very nice restaurant that I eat at quite a lot. I think you're going to enjoy it, Evie, Chez Victor's. There's a little something for everybody on their menu."

She smiled uncomfortably. It was starting to get peculiar, the fact that he had yet to mention Lucas, or the motel, or the argument from the night before. Why would her father save a conversation as potentially volatile as that for a place as public as a restaurant, one where they obviously knew him?

"You look really pretty today, Evie, you really do. Do you know that? Not too done up, natural-looking. The look suits you."

"Thank you, daddy."

They were on the highway now, the one that ran parallel to the old river road and the levee. She stared out the window and watched history fly by. She wondered what it might have looked like when her ancestors had ridden on that old road on horses and in carriages, most likely never dreaming of such a thing as a super highway, or even a car, for that matter. Part of her loved her ancestors dearly, even though all of them had been utter strangers to her. A place in her heart cherished them and loved the lives they had led.

Of course, there was always that blight of slavery that had made her family so difficult to talk about when she'd gone to school up north. There were years when she hated her ancestors for who they had been, and she'd tried hard to remove all hints of anything Southern from her mannerisms or the things she said.

And she'd hoped that when people saw her on the streets in town, off the school campus, that they'd just naturally assume she was a girl from up north, slave-free like everybody else. But now she didn't worry too much about it. Her family had been who they'd been and they were gone now and these were different times.

Evie wondered if the Amorys of Bywater had ever owned slaves or if they'd always been poor. She was curious to know about her father's old life and she hoped that one day soon he was going to tell her all about it. After all, he was the man her mother had loved enough to marry, to throw in her fortunes with. She must have wanted him, history and all.

Big Joe finally gave up the pretenses of small talk. He'd run out of things to say anyway. Soon enough they'd be getting closer to the city and he'd have to prepare her for the presence of the Harpers. He didn't want any more unpleasant surprises. He didn't want Evie to do or say anything unexpected that would only embarrass all of them.

He studied his daughter from the corner of his eye and wondered what it was she might be thinking about, staring out the window so intently like that. To him, even now, she still looked like a little girl. What could she have been thinking of, running off to that motel with Cain, he wondered. Cain was too old for her, too experienced, and she was so hopelessly naïve. What could they possibly do in a motel room together for so many hours?

But he had to wonder again if that was an accurate impression, that Evie was hopelessly naïve. Maybe it was all an act for his benefit. If it was, she certainly seemed to have Cal Harper fooled, too. Cal spoke of Evie as if she was a babe in the woods, but women had ways of creating illusions that could baffle even the worldliest of rogues.

Clarice could be the same way when she wanted to be, he remembered. She certainly had never given him any indication that she was despondent enough to kill herself, or clear-headed enough to have her estate in order before she took the pills, or shrewd enough to see to it that Vera would be kept on for life as Evie's watch guard within the vast DuMaret estate.

Big Joe forced himself to quit thinking about Clarice or about the suicide. It could only lead to another endless night without sleep. He couldn't afford that now. They were getting closer to the city anyhow. They were going to have to have that talk. "Evie, honey," he began, "I've invited Cal Harper and his father to have lunch with us today."

"What for?" she demanded.

"Cal has something he wants to discuss with you."

"I know Cal wants to marry me, daddy, I've known that all summer, but why are they coming to lunch? Why is he bringing his father?"

"To get better acquainted with you, that's all."

"I don't want to marry Cal, daddy. I don't need to get better acquainted with his father or any other Harper. I'm not in love with Cal, and he's not in love with me!"

"Of course he's in love with you, Evie."

"Daddy, he is not. If Cal Harper were in love with me, he wouldn't be so damn… I don't know, polite." She was starting to get the picture, and she felt outraged. No wonder there had been no mention of Lucas. Her father was trying to sweep it all under the rug and push through the issue of the Harpers as quickly as possible.

Thomas pulled the black Lincoln into the parking lot of Chez Victor's.

"I'm not going in there," Evie said. "This is crazy."

"You are going in there, and you're going to be polite. At least listen to the man, this is important to him. At least have a civilized lunch."

"I won't, daddy, there's no reason for it. This is a waste of everybody's time. I'm in love with Lucas Cain."

"Fine, Evie," he said calmly, "be in love with Lucas Cain, but you're not marrying Lucas Cain. You're marrying Cal Harper."

"I am not marrying Cal Harper!"

"You are, Evie, and you're going to pull yourself together and walk in that restaurant with me right now and start behaving like someone who has responsibilities. Be as gracious as everyone is expecting you to be. You know, Evie," he added, "there's a lot that goes along with being a DuMaret's descendent around here. It's about time you started acting like you have a clue what that entails."

Thomas had gotten out of the car and he held Evie's door open for her expectantly.

"Go on," her father said, nearly pushing her out the door.

"All right," she said through clenched teeth, not wanting to embarrass herself, "I'll have lunch and I'll be polite, but that's all."

Inside Chez Victor's, Cal and his father were already seated at a table. It was clearly the best table in the house, right next to a set of sparkling floor-to-ceiling French doors looking out across a beautiful sunny garden where an alabaster fountain burbled up gloriously. The room itself was dotted with towering palm trees that fanned out dramatically, showing off the domed ceiling. The highly polished black-and-white checked floor glistened in the streaming sunlight. Chez Victor's décor was subdued and elegant, the tables set with fine china and crystal stemware, the white linen cloths, spotless. The napkins at each place setting were intricately folded to resemble delicate water lilies, and the menu that supposedly held "a little something for everybody" apparently only included those "everybody's" who could afford to pay a cool fortune for the tiniest amounts of food imaginable.

Evie approached the table thinking that Cal and his father looked like a fortress of immovable twins, twins representing the North and the South. Cal was Harvard all the way. His education had been sophisticated and his travels abroad had been upper class and expensive. He wore his suit and tie like a man who relied on the supreme power of understatement to close a deal, and whose idea of frivolous would be to accessorize with cuff links or maybe a bow tie.

Mr. Harper, on the other hand, had been educated in Louisiana. He had been conceived, reared, molded and planted deep in the land that had produced his forebears. His tastes were more extravagant; he wasn't averse to the occasional flourish. One might spy the tip of a bright silk handkerchief poking up from his breast pocket, or the flash of a twenty-four karat gold watch peaking out from beneath his hand-tailored sleeve.

Together, they presented a forbidding pair. Evie wasn't eager to sit down with either of them.

"Evie," Cal said, rising slightly, "you look so pretty today, as always."

"Thank you, Cal," she countered, sounding remote and civilized. Gone was the easy camaraderie that had developed between them over the summer. Cal was the enemy, and she now saw that he always had been.

Mr. Harper was genial, but it was the false friendliness of a general who sees the imminent defeat of his opponent. In this case Evie, the young woman standing between his son and a fortune. She noted the refined, well-camouflaged greed surrounding her at the table. No one at the table – not even her own father – had been born as rich as she had.

And then it was like the crack of a delicate egg shell breaking open in her mind, only what came through the crack was the light of an idea she had never considered before. She had been born richer than all of them, and to stay rich, she hadn't had to lift a finger; she'd simply had to grow up. Greed had never entered her consciousness. In their world, Evie was the superior one, the foe they were trying to defeat. Her wealth was the sleeping monster they were hoping wouldn't awaken until they'd made off with all its riches. To men like these, being born the richest in the first place was what mattered, not how much wealth a person could acquire along the way. They would never be satisfied, these men. To those who hadn't been born the wealthiest, no amount of riches would ever be enough. It was good to accumulate wealth, certainly. It was good to acquire real estate, to earn interest on every dollar. It was a pastime that kept a person occupied as they spent their allotted days on earth. And acquiring what was rightfully Evie's would be the biggest coup of all.

Evie saw it now as though a great wind had come and blown everyone's masks away. This was serious business, this talk of marriage. For these men, love wasn't a factor at all. For her to reason or to plea would be meaningless. Love was just a word one pasted over the top of a marriage, but it had no place down in its foundation where the serious deals were struck.

She was outnumbered three-to-one. The best she could hope for would be to agree to all their grand plans, and then run like crazy when their backs were turned.

A crisp chardonnay was called for, ordered by Mr. Harper. "I don't think I ever had a chance to tell you, Evie," he said, "how truly stunning you looked at the party last month. You were quite a busy lady. I barely had time to speak with you at all."

The wine was offered, tasted, approved, and then poured around the table.

She watched her glass being filled and decided that a wine that looked as crisp and colorless as this one could only be palatable with cold, dead fish. "I was told I looked especially like my mother that night, Mr. Harper. Did you know my mother?"

Big Joe cringed. Clarice was the worst possible topic at a table like this.

"No, I never had the pleasure," Mr. Harper replied smoothly.

"She's where my money came from," Evie explained with a forced smile, ignoring her father's black-eyed glare. "It's funny, most people have heard of her but few seemed to have actually known her. A man who works for my father, Lucas Cain, seems to be one of the lucky ones who actually knew her. She died when I was born."

"Is that right?"

"Evie," Cal cut in clumsily, "I was hoping you might be free this evening. I was planning on taking a drive out to Solisville. I thought I might drop in on you."

"Yes, that's right," Evie went on, ignoring Cal. "My father can tell you, my mother died very young. An opportunity wasted; all that money and no time to spend any of it."

"Evie," her father cut in, "Cal asked you a question."

She sipped her wine and stared at Cal. "You're always welcome to drop in on me," she finally replied. "Have you got something on your mind?"

Big Joe and Mr. Harper eyed each other, and then all eyes were on Cal.

"The other night when you were over for dinner, you seemed

to have something on your mind," she went on, and then addressed the others. "Cal insisted on going for a walk in that sweltering heat wave, try as I did to dissuade him."

Mr. Harper gave a short laugh. "When you're young and in love, you don't notice things like oppressive heat. Isn't that right, Cal?"

Evie was struck by Cal's pained expression. He looked like he wanted to crawl under the table. She began to feel for sorry for him. Maybe she had misjudged what had been happening all summer. Maybe Cal was just as reluctant as she was to marry for money and not for love. Maybe he'd been dragged to this lunch just as she had. "When you're young," she corrected Mr. Harper graciously, "I suppose you don't notice a lot of things. Love has nothing to do with it."

Her father looked as though he wanted to ring her neck, but at least he couldn't fault her for her politeness.

The rest of the lunch was a stilted attempt to get Cal and Evie to behave as if they were birds of a feather, with so many untold things in common, their names born to be linked in at least every sentence, if not in outright matrimony. The pair of "love birds" settled amicably into an unspoken pact to at least get through lunch without either one succumbing to complete embarrassment, and after a light dessert, each agreed that a drive together later that evening might be just the thing they needed.

With Cal unexpectedly on her side, Evie found it effortless to be polite and charming to Mr. Harper. She said goodbye with a genuine smile.

"I'm sure we'll be seeing each other real soon," Mr. Harper said.

Evie smiled again knowing there wasn't a chance in hell they would.

Chapter Sixteen

The drive back to Solisville was tortuous. Evie's father was adamant that she keep her date with Cal for that evening.

"But Cal's no more interested in me than I am in him, at least when it comes to marriage."

"What's the harm in keeping the date? It's not as if you had anything else planned."

"How do you know I don't have anything else planned?"

"Well, I know for sure you're not seeing Lucas Cain. You might as well fill your time with somebody, so why not Cal?"

There it was finally, Lucas's name had come out of her father's mouth. It was hanging in the air in the back seat of the Lincoln, a deluge of anger poised to flood them just on the other side of it.

"And how would you know if I'm planning to see Lucas or not?"

"All I know is that Lucas isn't planning to see you, Evie, ever. He's ambitious. He knows a good thing when he's got one. He stands to take over the entire company if he plays his cards right, and he doesn't have time to toss it all away at this point in his life. It takes years of strategy to build a career. You're better off with someone more your own age whose goals in life are more in line with where yours are at right now."

Her father was talking crazy. How could he know any such thing about Lucas? "You don't have any idea what my goals are, daddy. How can you say something like that?"

"Maybe I don't really know you, Evie, that's true, and that's my fault, but I know my business, and I know Lucas Cain, and when he left the office this morning it was to re-think his goals with Donovan & Company, not his affair with you."

Affair? Evie had never considered the word before. The sound of it grated across her heart; it sounded so temporary, so inconsequential. "Is that what he told you?" She didn't believe it.

"More or less. Look, I'm sorry, Evie, Lucas Cain is a real ladies' man and I know he holds a certain appeal for you women. I'm not blind. But the fact of the matter is that you'd better not get your hopes up. I don't think Lucas is going to be calling on you anymore."

Disgusted, Evie stared out the window and refused to look at her father for the rest of the ride home. He didn't have a clue what he was talking about. Her father didn't know Lucas like she did. He didn't know the feelings there were between them. Lucas had probably said anything to appease her father, anything that would get him off his back and help him keep his job. But a sharp twinge of doubt blew her heart wide open. Hadn't it been Lucas himself who had said he never gave any thought to getting married? Hadn't he said his relationship with Evie could cost him his career and he wasn't willing to take that chance because his career was everything to him?

The thought that Lucas might value his relationship with her father more than what he had with her made Evie feel ill. And the comment her father had made about Lucas being a ladies' man, implying there were other women who were just as hot for Lucas, that thought made her skin crawl. Had Lucas been lying to her? Were there other women and other motel rooms? Or maybe he took the others to his own home, because they were women he didn't have to hide from Big Joe?

The drive to the house became endless. Evie wanted to get out and walk the rest of the way home, even though she knew it would be after sundown before she'd make it all that way on foot. She just couldn't stand sitting so close to her father, the enemy, the victorious enemy. More than anything, she wanted to be alone in her room.

***

The doorbell rang around half past six that evening. Evie heard it upstairs in her room, but she didn't budge to find out who it was. She didn't care.

A moment later, Vera was tapping at her door.

"What is it?" Evie called morosely.

"Evie, Cal Harper's downstairs. He says he has a date with you to go for a drive this evening."

"I'm not interested."

"Evie, that's rude. You come downstairs and speak to him."

Evie looked at herself in the mirror. How could she face anyone? She looked abysmal. She'd spent all afternoon locked in her room, bemoaning the situation with Lucas; her nerves couldn't stand the uncertainty of it. If her father turned out to be right, and Lucas could be through with her as easily as that, then she had made an unspeakable fool of herself.

"Evie, come on now." It was Vera again at the door. "You come out of there. Don't keep Cal waiting."

Vera was right; it was rude to just ignore Cal. It was a long drive from the city to their house up in Solisville and she had agreed to go out with him. She tried to fix her face and make herself a little more presentable. Although how she would disguise the ravages caused by a shattered heart remained a mystery.

Stop this, she reprimanded herself, Lucas is going to call. It isn't over yet. He's coming back. It hasn't even been twenty-four hours.

She chose a sophisticated black dress, hoping it made her look older, wiser even, like someone who hadn't made a common spectacle of herself over some man.

By the time she came downstairs and greeted Cal in the front room, she looked good enough to pass for a new and improved version of herself. "I'm sorry I kept you waiting," she said.

The Cal Harper who greeted her didn't seem to be in much better spirits than she was. In the same suit he'd had on all day, looking a bit the worse for wear, he had the air of a soldier making a gallant effort to rally the dying troops.

"Can I offer you anything, Cal? Did you eat yet?"

"I thought we might eat out, if that's okay with you?"

she grabbed her bag and they headed out to Cal's car, a two-door beige coup, not too sporty, understated but expensive, like everything else about Cal.

"I'm so sorry about that fiasco this afternoon, Evie," Cal began. He stuck his key in the ignition and then started the car. "This whole situation is so uncomfortable for me. You're such a great girl. I really like you."

"I like you too, Cal."

They drove a while in silence. Cal headed up the main road into Solisville. "How about the Tropical Breeze?"

"Sure," she agreed, not caring anymore if she was gawked at by everyone in town. She was getting used to feeling on display.

Sure enough, when she stepped foot into the restaurant, heads turned to look at her, and there was a general murmuring of recognition – a DuMaret was in their midst. Evie ignored it, but Cal seemed appreciative of all the attention.

When they were seated in a dark, quiet corner alone, he began all over again. "I guess you know that our fathers have been orchestrating this whole thing from the start."

"Yes, I know that," she said quietly.

"I assumed you did, even though we never really mentioned it to each other. You know, Evie, in the beginning I was angry for getting pressured to date somebody, anybody. I don't know how you felt about it, but I felt used by my old man. I've been making my own decisions for years. I don't need to be told who to date, you know? And this whole situation, it felt more like a business proposition than a social obligation."

"I know that, too. My father's tried arrangements like this before, but never with such determination."

"I guess that's understandable. I mean a woman like you has a lot of things to consider. You make a mistake and the repercussions could be so far reaching."

What did Cal mean by that?

"But you know what?" he went on. "In spite of all my initial objections, it turned out I really did like you. I wanted to date you. I spent the whole summer trying to get a rise out of you, trying to steer this… well, what is it? We're more than acquaintances, this relationship. I've been trying to steer this relationship with you into deeper waters, and you've resisted me at every turn. I know that you're selective, that a woman in your position has to be, but the fact remains, I really do like you."

Evie felt something stirring in her heart. Was it compassion? Cal really was a good sort.

"What happened at lunch today was so unnecessary, so forced. I apologize for it. I never should have agreed to show up at the restaurant, but then it never occurred to me that our fathers were up to something so tacky and medieval. I feel like all it did was set us back, you and me, you know, in trying to get to know each other. I guess I'm not really saying it right."

Evie felt a tiny ping of alarm. He's not really going to ask me...

"You're a woman of impeccable breeding, Evie, I could tell that the moment we met. You're beautiful and always a pleasure to be around. I made a half-assed attempt to talk to you about this the other night, and now I'm going to ask you again. I really would like to see more of you, Evie. I think we might have a lot in common. I think we might enjoy spending more time together, when that time isn't overshadowed by the agenda of our parents."

She wasn't sure what to say. She liked Cal, too, but she was hardly a woman of impeccable breeding. She couldn't see herself as this woman Cal was claiming he wanted so much to be around.

"If you give me a chance," he continued, "you never know, it might just turn out that we were meant to be together and everyone will be happy by default. And what's the worst that could come from it? We could wind up good friends."

Evie smiled. "Cal," she said, "I like you, too, and I'm willing to spend more time with you, casually. I can't promise anything more than that." She thought it was best to leave any mention of Lucas out of this. Why tell Cal that she was in love with someone else? He wasn't talking about commitments yet, he wasn't asking for something that required disclosure.

"Thanks, Evie, you've made me very happy. We might just rescue this atrocious day yet."

The air was suddenly lighter. The heavy burden of their fathers' wills had lifted. Cal and Evie enjoyed themselves finally. They took their time with the meal. They took pleasure in the luxury of their surroundings, even joking quietly between them about the many nosy patrons who were trying so hard not to stare at them while they ate.

After dinner, they took a short drive through the town of Solisville, and Evie played tour guide, showing Cal her father's television station, the offices of The Evening Call, and the office building where her father spent most of his time, the building where Lucas Cain had an office, as well, but she didn't tell Cal that part.

When Cal drove her home, it seemed natural that they should kiss goodnight. But it was a kiss between friends, nothing more, and she was relieved when he didn't pressure her to go further.

"I'll call you soon," he said.

She let herself in the house and she knew her father was still up, waiting for her in the front room, but she ignored him. She went upstairs to her room instead.

Chapter Seventeen

For the next few days, Lucas had work to do in the city, clients to check in on and new properties to investigate. He didn't go in to the Solisville office. He told himself it was better that way. He could sleep later by staying in the city, which was good, because he wasn't sleeping much at night. Lucas wouldn't admit it to himself, but he was slowly coming apart.

Luckily, he still had his work. From the time Lucas was a little boy, there was always work. It was what kept him sane in place of having love, having a loving person to turn to, a father let's say, or even a mother. Work kept his mind off the emptiness at home and gave him a sense of purpose. When he was ten-years-old, he got his first job sweeping up after school in a run down corner grocery in Bywater for fifty cents an hour. Getting a paycheck made Lucas feel like he actually mattered for the first time in his life. From then on, when there was work, Lucas knew he had value.

Lucas never knew his father, in fact no one was sure who Lucas's father was, not even his mother had known for sure. There had been so many men that she'd never bothered to speculate, and she didn't stick around long enough to see which old flame Lucas might grow up to look like.

Of course, "old flame" was just a euphemism for what had really gone on in his mother's bedroom, the room right next to Lucas's separated only by a single hollow door. Shotgun houses were like that, no privacy to speak of. Room followed room until you were right out the back door, and double shotguns were worse, the kind of house Lucas had grown up in. It meant that another complete household was only one wall away.

Lucas's mother, Corinna Cain, had been just sixteen when Lucas was born. The house they lived in, as meager as it was, had actually been a Godsend. Corinna never had to pay one penny of rent on account of her special relationship with the landlord. It was that very same landlord that helped Lucas land his first job.

Corinna was a very beautiful girl, everyone said so, dark hair, dark eyes, long legs, fine high cheek bones and a figure out of some high fashion magazine. The whole block knew it was just a matter of time and Corinna's ship would come in. Poor girls who looked like Corinna, who were willing to accommodate all sorts of unusual masculine tastes, didn't stay poor girls for long.

When her ship did come in, it was in the shape of a man named Mr. Caster. He was in New Orleans on a business trip from Savannah. Corinna was twenty-eight-years-old at the time, in her physical prime. If a ship were ever going to come and get her, that would be the time. There wasn't time left for any more chances. "If he'd come a day later," she'd told Lucas, "that over-the-hill business would be starting to show."

When Corinna took off with Mr. Caster, she wished Lucas a

lot of luck. And as it turned out, he sure needed it. That was when Lucas was twelve. He tried to stay on alone in the house, but the dollar an hour he was earning by then couldn't pay the rent, and the landlord had no special arrangements he could make with a boy like Lucas. But the landlord was instrumental in finding Lucas a situation that would 'pay' in room and board. It was at a call house on Royal Street, in the Vieux Carré, not far from Bywater. Miss Willie was the proprietress. She was a shrunken old black woman whose primary calling in life had been that of Voodoo Mother, but she turned her holy temple into a call house after a run in with some bad medicine landed her a stint in jail. It was easier to pay off nosy cops with an hour or two of a free girl than it was to pay them off when it was just stinking Voodoo. Who needed that?

So Miss Willie ran her call house without much interference from the authorities and her flair for hiring beautiful women of all ethnic backgrounds gave her house a reputation for the off-beat, and as such attracted a lucrative clientele. You didn't have to want sex to come hang at Miss Willie's. All kinds of vices were welcome, even encouraged. There was always a good poker game going on, among other up-all-night things. And rooms could be rented discreetly for an evening that didn't have to include any of Miss Willie's girls.

It was Lucas's responsibility to keep the place clean, to run the errands, and to fetch things for customers, whatever was required. Lucus didn't mind the work because he met such interesting people, but it bothered him that he never actually got paid. He was paid in room and board only, and any tips the customers felt inclined to toss his way.

Of course, with hours like the ones Miss Willie kept, school was out of the question. Lucas dropped out illegally, but there was no one around to care enough to notice that he was truant for an entire year. After that, there was no more record of Lucas Cain in the public school system. He'd gone on officially to the working life.

Lucas stayed on with Miss Willie until she got too old to be running a call house and she shut it down. By then she was rich anyway, so she didn't care. But in those few years that Lucas was with her, Miss Willie tried to take good care of him, and when it was time for him to move on, she found him another job. It wound up being a turning point for Lucas. It was a job looking after a woman's house, just a house, not a call house, a place where the woman lived. But she was rich and she wanted companionship that could be trusted. She was willing to pay by the week for that person's trust. That woman was Lucille, and Lucille helped Lucas get an equivalent of a high school diploma. She gave him a lot of books to read and taught him about the importance of making a good first impression. Lucille kept Lucas in very fine clothes, teaching him the difference between tailored and off-the-rack. Lucas was 'kept' and he was okay with it. He knew it was generally known by Lucille's friends that he shared the same bed as Lucille, but he was getting a weekly paycheck and an education, to boot. He drove a fancy car, wore fine clothes and lived in a big old house. He was on top of the world.

Whenever he felt as if his inner life were lacking, when the long empty nights were making him panic and his world was heading for a tailspin, Lucas looked at that paycheck and he knew he had value. He knew that one day what Big Joe Donovan had told him once would pay off, that staying poor was a choice, not a life sentence, and everyday Lucas was choosing not to stay poor.

And it had paid off. Lucas wasn't poor anymore. In fact, now he worked for Big Joe, he was second in command, poised to take over the works when Big Joe finally felt like retiring, or when he finally kicked off to the sweet hereafter to claim his great reward. But now when the long empty nights were making Lucas panic, a quick glance at his financial holdings didn't go too far in helping him fall back to sleep. What was there, though, if not work? How else could he measure his success, or know that he mattered? What did other people do to feel like they mattered? They spread their money around, if they had any, and acted like big shots. Or some people drank a lot. Other people had sex with the first person who'd say yes. But none of those people ever seemed very happy. And when he tried to imagine what it might feel like to be happy, he couldn't help but think of Evie.

But that was no good. He knew the score. Evie was an heiress, she was from another world a world he had seen before, even if it was only from afar. But he was familiar enough with it to know that rich people might go slumming from time to time, but they rarely did what Clarice DuMaret had done; they rarely crossed over and made commitments to those in the lower classes.

That's what it really came down to for Lucas, a class system.

Who was Evie Donovan? She was too young to know what society would soon be demanding of her, a certain propriety, an adherence to an unspoken code of the rich. She was part of the upper class and they would eventually completely claim her; Donovan was going to see to that. And Lucas was the bastard son of a whore. There were peaks he could still scale, things he could achieve with his kind of pedigree, especially in Donovan's empire where a good first impression went a long way. On the surface, most people assumed a lot, even Evie had assumed Lucas had gone to college, but what would she think of him if she knew the truth of his education, if she knew about Lucille?

Evie was just too beautiful, lovelier even than Clarice had been, because she was unspoiled by bitterness, she wasn't jaded, and she wasn't looking to escape herself. Not yet, anyway, and Lucas sincerely hoped she would never come to that. To expose Evie to the kinds of things he'd been a part of or the debasing things he'd seen… How would love survive the gutter? His own mother had showed him that in the gutter there was no love, only money.

Money Lucas could get anywhere. He didn't need to trouble Evie for money. But love, what was that? Whenever he tried to think about love, only two ideas came to him – that love led to obsessive behavior, and that only work, not love, could sustain his soul. Besides, rich or poor, Evie Donovan was too young and still impressionable, susceptible to making irreversible mistakes. And just like Lucas's young mother had, Evie might grow to resent her mistakes and leave him.

***

As the days passed and there was still no word from Lucas, Evie slipped deeper into despair. She managed to keep up her appearance for the sole reason that she wanted to look as pretty as possible if Lucas dropped by unannounced, but it took a lot of effort keeping her ravaged heart from showing on her face.

She couldn't keep from jumping each time the phone rang or from running to the window whenever a car came up the drive, but the only car that ever came up the drive was the black Lincoln.

She obsessed about the time Lucas had come by unexpectedly in the middle of the night and tossed those pebbles at her window. It could happen again, she thought, and that thought kept her awake a night, kept her ears straining at every sound. She didn't want to be dead to the world when her lover finally came back to her.

If Big Joe had felt like the enemy before, he had now advanced to the rank of brutal conqueror, his aggressive defeat of Evie's happiness growing to mythic proportions in her mind. It was true, she realized, everything about her father came down to money. If he had once married a young woman named Clarice DuMaret for love, he seemed to have forgotten all about it. Passion, desire, need, these weren't commodities traded on the open market so they had fallen from her father's awareness, if they had ever been there at all.

Evie's roiling hatred of her father only forced her feelings for her mother to the opposite extreme, towards the sublime. She felt certain that if her mother were still alive she would be on Evie's side, that love would matter above all.

She refused to speak to her father. What few meals she ate, she took either alone in her room or in the kitchen with the help. She made certain she didn't get out of bed until he'd left for work in the morning, and she tried to keep out of sight when he came home at night.

"You're killing your father, you know that?" Vera said. "He's only trying to do what's best for you in the long run." It was early evening and the rest of the help was gone. Vera was putting the last of the dinner dishes away in the kitchen pantry. Evie's father wasn't expected home until at least midnight. He was having his dinner out. For all Evie knew, he was having his dinner in a fancy restaurant with Lucas Cain in tow, forcing Lucas onto some client's reprehensible wife.

Evie was seething. Why did Vera always have to take her father's side? It hadn't always been like that. At this hour of the evening, the kitchen was usually at its most serene. The setting sun cast a peaceful shadow over the room. It was Vera's favorite spot to hide away in after the day help had gone home. For some reason, tonight Evie had sought Vera out like she had in the old days, when she was a little girl home from boarding school. Back then Vera had been her confidant. They would sit in the kitchen together and talk for hours. Evie's father was never keen on television, even though he owned the small TV station in town. He wanted Evie to use her mind not waste it, to think about things, to read, to converse or listen to music. Vera whole-heartedly supported Big Joe's wishes, and she helped Evie find many creative ways to pass the time when she was home from school. But that was a long time ago.

"It seems like just yesterday, doesn't it," Vera went on, as if reading Evie's mind, "we used to sit here together and talk. Remember, Evie? I miss those days. But I guess everybody has to grow up."

The kitchen was an enormous open room that ran the full width of the back of the house. Because of its age, its having been built long before air conditioning was so much as dreamed of, it was a well-ventilated room. It's windows, on all three sides, were actually enormous French doors that opened onto side porches and the back patio. The kitchen had a low-beamed ceiling, painted white, and the original handmade brick floor. It had its original brick fireplace, too, set deep into the wall, its hearth running clear to the ceiling. The fireplace was big enough to stand in. It was where all the cooking had been done in the house's early days. When Evie was little, she used to stare at that fireplace and try to imagine all the thousands of meals that had been cooked there by people who were now long gone.

Today, the kitchen was fully modern, equipped with the same

state-of-the art gadgets found in other rich people's kitchens, but it had managed to retain its inviolate aura of security and home. It was clearly the heart of the house and always had been. A large butcher-block kitchen table was at the center of the room, and here is where Vera sat in the evenings, usually drinking a cup of tea. It's where Vera and Evie had sat together in earlier days, and where Vera and Clarice had sat together before that. In all, Vera had spent most evenings at that kitchen table for nearly forty years.

Evie wondered now why she had bothered to come to Vera. She should have known better. Thick as thieves, that's how she thought of Vera and her father these days. "What is it with you two anyway?" Evie blurted out. "Why are you always against me? It didn't used to be that way."

"We're not against you," Vera sighed. She set a pot of water on the stove to boil. It was time for her tea. "We're just trying to look out for your best interests, that's all. Can't you understand that it killed your father, and me, to lose your mother the way we did? We just don't want it to happen again."

That didn't make any sense. "But she died in childbirth, Vera. It's not like a person can avoid that by marrying a man like Cal Harper instead of Lucas Cain."

Vera realized too late that she'd slipped up. "You know, Evie, this feud going on between you and your father is really wearing me out. The tension around here is thick. I can't take it. Why can't you two agree to disagree and at least try to get along?"

"Agree to disagree? Are you crazy? We're talking about my future here, Vera. He wants me to marry a man I'm not in love with. And the man I am in love with isn't allowed anywhere near me or he'll lose his job! I don't see any middle ground there, do you?"

Vera sat down at the kitchen table and was silent.

Evie thought she looked old, and was surprised she'd never noticed it before. She sat down at the table with her suddenly feeling sorry for Vera. Her whole life had been that house, that table. First she had raised Evie's mother, and then she had raised Evie. "What did you mean by that?" Evie was suddenly back to Vera's comment about Clarice. "What happened to my mother that you don't want to see happen again?"

Vera's whole body seemed to sag in defeat.

"What is it, Vera? Aren't you feeling okay?"

"Evie, I'm so tired. I'm tired of watching you suffer when it's supposed to be for your own good. I'm tired of disagreeing with your father, but having to present this united front in order to do what's best for you. But you know what? You're going to be twenty-two years old soon. You need to live your own life, and I suppose that includes making your own mistakes, even if they're big ones. Maybe they won't be. It's not as though your father can fire me for speaking my mind."

Now Evie was more confused than ever. She'd never heard Vera talk like this.

"It seems like all he's managing to do with this line of thinking," Vera went on, "is drive a wedge between you two. He's pushing you away. It only stands to reason that you'll eventually leave. Why should you stay? You're old enough to be on your own, you have more money than you'll probably ever spend. In fact, I don't know why you are staying if you love this man so much."

Evie was dumbfounded. "You want me to leave, to move out?"

"No, honey, I don't, but I also don't understand why you haven't already, except for the fact that your father has kept you as helpless as he possibly could your whole life. But even you,

Evie, have managed to summon a bit of that DuMaret spirit these last few months."

There was something a little insulting in that last remark, but Evie wasn't sure what it was. "What do you mean that even I'm managing to do it?"

"The DuMarets were feisty people, Evie, nobody ever pushed a DuMaret around. I'm not telling you that you should rebel against your father. I'm not saying that at all, I'm just saying that for someone with DuMaret blood, you're very docile. You might look just like her, Evie, but I don't think your own mother would have recognized you as a DuMaret."

"What are you talking about? She was the most fragile of all–"

"She was not fragile, Evie." Vera almost sounded disgusted. The water was boiling and she got up to make her tea. "Clarice was anything but fragile. I'm going to tell you something, Evie, and your father will probably never forgive me for saying this, but your mother loved life. She took life by the horns as soon as she was old enough to walk. She drove your grandparents out of their minds. Your grandfather used to say that Clarice had sent her mother to an early grave with all her wild ways. That was an exaggeration, but unfortunately it proved to be true for your grandfather; your mother did help him to an early grave. Your mother was practically incorrigible she was so misbehaved, but it was because she was in a hurry to live life to the fullest, like every DuMaret had been before her. And she died because she realized too late that she was no longer in control of her life, that some-body else was pulling the strings. She chose to die rather than live life like a slave to anybody or anything. No, Evie, your mother was far from fragile."

It was as if Vera were talking about another person entirely. This was not a Clarice Evie had ever heard of before. "You mean she died because she didn't want to be a mother? She didn't want a baby pulling her strings?"

"Evie, you had nothing to do with why your mother died."

"What do you mean?"

"Your mother died because she made what she thought was an irreversible mistake." Vera sat down next to Evie at the table. "This notion that your mother died in childbirth was just something that was said to save face, to keep the gossipmongers at bay. I know this is going to hurt, honey, but it's time you knew the truth. Then maybe you'll understand why your daddy is so protective of you, why he's tried so hard to steer you in your decisions. The truth is, your mother killed herself, Evie, right after you were born."

It didn't make a sound the crack that shattered Evie's world, but she felt the full force of it as it cut through her heart. "She killed herself?" she repeated softly. "You're sure?"

"Oh, we're sure, honey, she left a note. Your father still has it somewhere. She wrote him a letter and left it on his pillow."

"How did she do it?"

"She took sleeping pills."

"But why would she want to die? She had everything, money, love, a family, a big house, and she was beautiful." Evie felt too stunned to cry. Something in her heart gave way now like an avalanche, and then there was only emptiness in that place, that place inside her where she used to keep her mother. There was no Clarice DuMaret, at least not the one she had been told about. There was instead this other one, this feisty, self-centered stranger. "How could she do it?" she pleaded with Vera. "How could any woman kill herself when she'd just had a baby?"

"She did it because she was trying to save you."

"Me?"

"She was trying to save you from her mistakes. Evie, your mother was in a deep depression. She was young and she was scared and apparently she thought she was all alone with no one else to turn to. If she had come to me, I would have told her to get a divorce, plain and simple, but I guess the idea wasn't so simple to her. She was afraid of your father, afraid of the man he was back then."

"She was afraid of my father? Of daddy? If she was so afraid of him, why did she leave me alone with him?"

"She didn't, Evie, she left you with me. She left the house with him. Your mother thought I would be better at protecting you than she would have been. She thought she'd made a mess of her life." Vera heaved a sorrowful sigh. "And you know, Evie, maybe she had. She made a big mess of a lot of things, but she shouldn't have blamed herself like she did. She had help making that mess."

The sun was nearly gone from the sky. Vera got up and turned on the kitchen light.

The room that was so familiar to Evie had a different history now. The whole house did. Her mother had suffered in it, had taken her own life in that house, and she had never known. She wanted to kill her father. "Why did he lie to me?" she cried. "And if he was so bad that my own mother didn't want to live anymore, why did you let him stay? Why didn't you throw him out after my mother died?"

Like a dam that had been threatening to burst for a hundred years, Vera brought on the deluge. At last, she decided to tell Evie the whole story.

Chapter Eighteen

Clarice DuMaret, dressed to the nines, was coming out of Antoine's late one summer night. The bottle of Ch,teauneuf-du-Pape she'd shared with a friend over dinner had left her head feeling appealingly light. On the narrow sidewalk outside the famous restaurant, a man was passing as Clarice came out the door. He was dark and tall. Clarice, already in an enchanted frame of mind, found his dark good looks captivating. She'd never seen a man quite like him. He spoke to Clarice. He knew her by name, but then a lot of people did. After all, she was a DuMaret.

"How are you tonight, Clarice?" the stranger asked with a smile. "Do you always look this pretty or are you celebrating something?"

"Right now I'm celebrating being alive," Clarice replied. "Later on, I'll probably still be celebrating that very same thing. It's what I do."

Something in the man's eyes perked up when she spoke, as if what Clarice was saying had great import. "Well, that sounds like a lovely way to pass an evening," he said. "I wouldn't mind celebrating being alive. It's been a while since I did that."

"You should try to do it at least a little bit everyday."

"If I were with a lady like you, Clarice, I know for sure I would celebrate a little bit everyday, at the very least." And then the tall dark stranger asked Clarice for the pleasure of her company right there and then. He wanted to take her out somewhere, to celebrate life, to have a drink on him.

"And what's your name?" she asked him.

"Joseph Donovan," he replied.

"And don't you think it's a little late, Joseph Donovan, to be asking a lady out for a drink?"

"If the bars are still open, and your eyes are still open, then it's not too late."

Clarice accepted, and together they set out on the old narrow streets of the French Quarter in search of something more sophisticated than Joseph's usual holes-in-the-wall.

An after dinner drink in the bar of a modest hotel turned into a sunrise over by the embankment of the Mississippi. Clarice and Joseph, their sleepy heads getting romantically close, strolled outside Jackson Square as the sky grew light and an early morning mist settled down around the Vieux CarrÈ. More than anything, Joseph wanted to invite Clarice up to his room, to come home with him, to come to his bed, but you didn't invite a girl from one of the richest families in New Orleans up to a cheap rented room. And yet it was five a.m., and he couldn't just leave her, but what was he supposed to do with her? He did the polite thing and offered to see her home.

"I have a house over on Elysian Fields," she said.

He was shocked. "You do?" He would have expected a much fancier address.

"I do. I bought it a couple of years ago, much to the chagrin of my father, but I wanted a place of my own in the city. I get tired of being stuck up there in Solisville. It's a pretty funky place, my house. You want to come see it?"

Joseph jumped at the opportunity. This wasn't just a chance to escort her home, this was an invitation to come inside.

Clarice lived alone, no roommates, no hired help. Joseph was on his best behavior, treating her like a queen. When he seduced her, it was with subtlety and finesse. He was hoping to win her confidence, but what he got was her complete trust, in spades. Clarice invited him to her bed, where she made love with a man for the first time.

Before long, within a month actually, Joseph gave up his rented room and was living in the house on Elysian Fields. Joseph Donovan, Big Joe as he was called, came from the street. His crawl spaces included smelly dives along Bourbon Street, rotting absinthe houses, shacks out on Bayou St. John, and the occasional tĺte-‡-tĺte in a pirogue on the cypress swamps. He had no formal education. He learned by watching people. He was thirty-three-years-old when he met Clarice DuMaret and by then he'd watched a lot of questionable people doing a lot of shady things.

One thing Big Joe loved to do was play poker. When his mojo was working, he could make a decent living going from game to game. When he met Clarice, he was on a roll, and that roll lasted for a couple of years. Clarice was a veritable good luck charm, if not an outright bankroll.

No one could accuse Clarice of being a shrew, or of being anything less than a good sport, a woman who took life head on and wasn't afraid of a gamble. It was part of the DuMaret spirit. She loved ideas. She loved life. She was generous to a fault and could afford to be. Clarice had an impressive monthly allowance and stood to inherit a staggering fortune one day, most of it in real estate. Like all the DuMaret women, she had been raised like southern royalty, but she avoided the fast international set, girls she had gone to school with. She found their hard-hearted competitiveness grating. She sought out, instead, a more free-spirited recklessness, which she soon discovered could in itself be a thrilling high and as addictive as a drug. And no one knew the fine art of recklessness like Big Joe for the simple fact that he had never had anything to lose.

Big Joe and Clarice made a fantastic pair, everyone thought so, everyone wanted to join the party that Big Joe and Clarice created wherever they went. It was true that Clarice was no stranger to misbehaving before she met Joseph Donovan, but he taught her an impressive array of vices. It was his insatiable carnal appetites that tore her purse strings wide open, and things she had never dreamed of doing in the past – for instance drinking expensive vintage champagne solely to take the edge off the unnerving effects of too much cocaine – gradually became common place in her life. And the house on Elysian Fields became filled with fine things. Clarice had bought them for Big Joe; she was known to approve of everything when it came to love, and that's what it was between Clarice and Big Joe – love.

He accepted her, encouraged her quirky nature, her flights into the fantastic with the aid of more and more high-priced drugs, and she accepted him. She had given him her virginity, hadn't she? They were going to be married. She encouraged everything that made him happy, even his high stakes gambling, reveling in his winnings as much as he did.

When it came to sex, Joseph taught Clarice everything, until they were both a couple of live wires. They were incapable of exhausting each other try as they might. Their marathon lovemaking sessions, held in one of Miss Willie's upstairs rooms, were legendary. The two could go and go and go. Of course, without the help of expensive drugs and champagne, it might have been a different story, but the pair never bothered to experiment with sobriety.

It was rumored that Big Joe knew a good thing when he had one and that his taste for poker was more pronounced than his love for Clarice, but no one called him on it. At the very least, they were inseparable companions. That much was obvious to anybody. When Clarice wound up pregnant, Big Joe did right by her and insisted they get married, even though it was also rumored that the father could have been any of a number of men. To celebrate the marriage, Big Joe and Clarice lived it up, ironically, in a rank dive called the Hi Life Motel.

But things soured when Clarice took Joseph Donovan up to Solisville to meet Mr. DuMaret. Clarice's father had already gotten wind of how she'd been behaving around the Quarter, and he'd seen the bills for his new son-in-law's expensive tastes. He refused to sanction the marriage. He threatened to cut Clarice off if she didn't file for an annulment.

"But I'm having a baby!" Clarice argued. "I need a husband!"

Mr. DuMaret took this to mean that the husband wasn't necessarily the father of this unfortunate pregnancy, and the degree to which his daughter had ruined her life sent the old man into a frenzy of rage that culminated in a quick but very fatal heart attack.

***

"After your grandfather died," Vera explained, "your parents moved up here to the house and I stayed on to look after your mother. Her own mother had died when she was in her early teens, and no woman wants to be alone, without another woman, I mean, during a pregnancy, especially her first one. I saw everything fall apart. Your mother tried to make sense of what was happening. Your father was frequently gone for several days at a time, reappearing only when he was low on funds, then she tried to make the best of it, but she was facing the harrowing task of trying to stay clean and sober while she was carrying you. I think it was too much. On one of the rare times he was home, I tried to convince your father that Clarice needed psychiatric help, at least to get her through the emotional upheaval of losing her father and having her first baby, but he seemed to think your mother could handle anything."

Evie's heart felt raw. Perhaps if she'd been told this version of her parents' lives in smaller doses over the course of several years, it would have been easier to stomach, but as it was, in one sitting… she felt like she was going to be sick.

"After your mother killed herself, Evie, your father fell to pieces. To this day he has never stopped blaming himself. And he has tried so hard to make sure you'd turn out different, that you'd have a shot at a better life than your mother had."

"But it sounds to me like there's a good chance he isn't even my father."

"Evie, don't say that. He loved your mother and he married her and he raised you. That counts for everything."

Evie wasn't so sure. What counted was that he'd wound up with at least part of her mother's inheritance, and he took that part and grew it into an empire. In Evie's opinion, her father didn't seem to have suffered too much.

"Don't be too hard on him, Evie." Vera knew there would be hell to pay now. The rift between Evie and Big Joe was only going to get worse. She had hoped it would go the other way, and maybe it still would, when Evie had had time to digest it all, to think. At least maybe now she would understand why her father did the things he did. "Don't you see, Evie that this fellow Lucas Cain is too much like your father for him to feel comfortable about it? In your father's eyes, it's as if history were getting ready to repeat itself. He wants you to be safe, your future to be secure. He wants you to be with someone of your own kind, not someone from the street."

"Lucas Cain is not from the street! He may have been poor, but that doesn't mean his home was a nest of vipers or anything. He had a mother, you know. He's a human being. He has a good job."

"But come on, Evie he took you to a motel and he kept you there until all hours. That's indecent! Would a man like Cal Harper, a man with a good upbringing, ever suggest doing a thing like that?"

"Cal Harper knows a thing or two about life, Vera. He's been all over the world. I'm sure he's been in a motel room with a woman at one time or another."

Vera gave up. She got up from the table. Her joints were stiff from having sat there so long. "I know you can understand the point I'm trying to make, Evie, you just don't want to. I'm sorry for all of this, I really am. I know you're upset and I just hope you're going to be able to forgive us. As for the rest of it, I guess the chips are just going to have to fall where they may."

Chapter Nineteen

Forgiveness was a word Evie gave a lot of thought to in the days that followed Vera's bombshell.

October was rapidly approaching and the more comfortable weather had come. Evie spent a lot of time out in the garden alone, or on the porch, sitting in the swing.

She didn't try to avoid her father anymore. It was more that she simply didn't see him whenever he was there. She looked right through him. She wouldn't speak to him. If he spoke to her, she acted as if she hadn't heard.

Forgiveness? Evie didn't think it was going to be likely. The way she saw it, her father – if that was indeed who he was – had taken everything from her, starting with her mother and ending with her lover, and everything in between.

Lucas Cain never did call again. Evie toyed with the idea of driving over to her father's office and confronting Lucas, but she didn't want to make a spectacle of herself. She didn't want to give her father the satisfaction of watching her be humiliated by a man he had wound up understanding better than she did. And mostly she didn't want to be anymore of a fool for Lucas than she'd already been. If he was more interested in a lousy job, than so be it.

But what she still couldn't come to terms with was how her heart could have been so wrong.

Cal Harper came to call on her more frequently, as he'd said he would, but now they were clearly at cross-purposes. Cal was angling toward marriage regardless of the things he'd tried to convince her of at dinner. But who knew for sure? Maybe she was being too hard on Cal; maybe he really was feeling amorous enough toward her to want to marry her, but all she wanted now was a friend, someone to confide in, and she quickly surmised that it couldn't be Cal.

Besides, what would Cal think if he knew the truth about Evie's parents, that her father had been poor or that he might not be Evie's father at all? Conservatism was the lifeline of Cal's family. Knowing who she really was now, where she came from… she just couldn't see anything good coming from an engagement to Cal Harper. And besides, it was like a broken record in her brain – she was in love with Lucas, try as she did to hate him.

Late one night after Cal had dropped her back home after a dinner date, an exhausted Evie tapped on Vera's bedroom door.

Vera was still awake. "Who is it?" she called.

"It's me, Evie."

Vera was never so relieved. She let Evie in and begged her to sit down with her on the bed. She took Evie's hands in hers. Her tired eyes were edged with tears. "Evie, I'm so glad you finally came to speak with me. I've been giving it a lot of thought, some of those things I said. I've been losing sleep over all of it."

Evie broke down like a little baby. "Vera, I don't know what to do. I don't want to live like this anymore. I hate this place. I hate being anywhere near my father, but I don't know where else to go. I know I don't have a life of my own. Don't you think I know that better than anybody? I never figured out how to have one. I don't know how to be a DuMaret. The only time I was ever truly happy, the only time I ever felt like I was strong and could be myself, like I was making my own decisions, was when I was with Lucas. And I just don't understand why he doesn't want me. I'm still so in love with him, Vera. I've tried to stop loving him, but I can't." It was like everything she'd been trying to deny was finally coming out, full force and without mercy. Her heart ached as she sobbed miserably.

Vera put her arms around Evie and held her. Vera felt like she had made so many mistakes. She'd contributed to this mess just as much as Evie's father had by going along with him all these years, and then with all this marriage talk. "You know, honey, if a man is decent and kind and has a good upbringing like Cal Harper, well, those things are good qualities, but they don't make a marriage. I could kick myself for ever having told you things like that. I can't see what would have been so wrong with Lucas Cain. The more I thought about it as I laid awake in bed, the more I realized your mother would never have approved of Cal Harper in a million years, unless that's who you were truly in love with. It would have gone against everything she believed in. And here I was, entrusted with your care, and I think I let her down. I know I let you down. It's more important now that you look at yourself, at who you are. You don't even know what you're capable of yet. The world should be your oyster, Evie. I know that's what your mother would have wanted. You haven't had a chance to find out who you are. You shouldn't even be thinking about marrying anyone strictly because they'd make good investments for you! That's just so crazy, I don't know why I didn't see it before, but that's really what your father has this idea of marriage boiled down to. You know," she went on, "there's still the house on Elysian Fields."

"What do you mean?"

"Your mother's house. It's still there. Your father owns it. That's where my mother stayed. She lived there with a nurse until she died a few years ago. It's been closed up for awhile, but it wouldn't take much to make it livable again. You could have your own life. You could think things through."

A home of her own… it was a like a Godsend. It was what Evie had been praying for. "You really think my father would let me have that house?"

Vera didn't hesitate. "I'll make sure he does," she promised her. "Your mother would have wanted it that way."

***

It took nearly a month to make the house on Elysian Fields habitable again. Any communications about the house were done through Vera, who was just about at her wit's end. "You've got to talk to your daughter," she told Big Joe. "Don't you realize she's leaving you? Are you going to let her move out from here, her home, her family's home, harboring such bad feelings? You've got to say something to her. You've got to at least try."

"What's left?" he countered bitterly. "It seems to me that you said all there was to say."

"You know it wasn't fair, Joseph. Someone had to tell her. That poor girl was going out of her mind."

Underneath his thick skin, Big Joe felt like he'd failed his daughter, like he'd yet again failed Clarice. And to make matters worse, Lucas Cain was slipping up at the office. His heart didn't seem to be in his work anymore. Who was going to be Big Joe's right hand man if Cain didn't work out? Everything in his world was changing, his carefully thought out plans were falling apart. His whole life, Big Joe had always been making arrangements for everything to eventually work out all right, and he had no contingency plan in place for when it didn't.

He couldn't bring himself to talk to Evie. He couldn't face how he now looked in his daughter's eyes. He was the reason her mother was dead. He knew she thought that; he knew she blamed him.

On the moving day, there was no big truck, no boxes to load. Evie was leaving everything behind except for her clothes. She was starting new, a new life, in a house that it broke Big Joe's heart to so much as step foot in. I should have sold that old rat trap years ago, he told himself now. What's going to happen to her there?

What could happen? Would she be consumed by the ghosts? Would she find out more than she'd already learned from Vera? There wasn't anymore to tell. All the secrets were out.

Big Joe got in the back of the Lincoln and told Thomas to take him to work. He didn't even tell Evie goodbye.

Chapter Twenty

Lucas looked at himself in the bathroom mirror. Was it his imagination, or was he looking old as hell? What a vision to kick-off his morning.

As he picked out a suit from his closet, he made a mental checklist of the things he was going to do. He was going to get a decent night's sleep one of these days. He was going to quit wandering the streets of the Quarter and hanging out in bars. He was going to renew his efforts at the office.

He needed to re-think a lot of things. He'd begged off too many meetings lately. Lucas knew he was on thin ice at the office, but he couldn't stand the sight of Donovan's face anymore. What was he supposed to do about that? What was the point in avoiding work, though? What was the point in all this wandering?

The point, he reminded himself on his way downstairs, was to keep himself from getting into his car at night and driving out to see Evie. The point was to stay the hell out of Solisville whenever possible. The point was to pull himself together.

He skipped breakfast. He went outside and got in his car. He stuck his key in the ignition. And then he sat there.

What is the point, he asked himself again. What is the point?

***

The house on Elysian Fields was a bit rundown, but Evie thought it was charming. She saw right away why her mother had bought it. It was something Evie understood in her bones. It was a one- and-a-half story cottage one room wide made entirely from cypress wood, and it had stood on that little spot since the eighteen-sixties. It had four rooms on the first floor, one after another, and a small curved stairway at the back of the house that led up to a single small bedroom. In front, the house sat practically on the street, but in back there was an old courtyard hidden inside a jungle-like garden. That was where Evie spent most of her days, lost in thought and hidden from the world.

At night, she wandered the four downstairs rooms. She was at a bit of a loss, never having been on her own before. She wasn't quite sure what to do with herself, her time, or the thoughts that were in her head. So she wandered from creaky room to creaky room and then back again, until she was tired enough to go to sleep.

Mostly, she thought about her mother. She tried to piece together a new idea of who that woman had been. And even though so many of the things that had come to light about Clarice DuMaret Donovan were hardly flattering to her, Evie found this new Clarice easier to picture. She was at last a three dimensional person Evie knew for sure had actually lived. It was as if the old Clarice had been a mere outline, an idea that had never fully formed, whereas this new Clarice contained the unmistakable spark that had once been a woman's life.

Nights in the little house on Elysian Fields were haunting. It was then that the essence of once-lived lives made themselves known, not so much as actual ghosts, but as phantoms that haunted Evie's mind. She found herself envious of her parents once again, for the apparent gusto with which they'd lived their lives. Curiously, Evie began to think of her father in the past tense, too, as if the man he'd really been had perished along with her mother when she'd killed herself. She felt both their wild and wicked lives endured somehow, eternally together, in that little cottage on Elysian Fields.

According to legend (or at least to what Vera had said) Clarice had been a virgin when she'd moved into the little house and Joseph Donovan had been chosen the lucky man to deflower her.

Evie wondered which room it had been in, the little room at the top of the strange curving stairway or the room downstairs where she herself slept?

Of course she couldn't help but be reminded of Lucas then, and how it had felt to at last come alive down there between her legs. Maybe Clarice had sown too many wild oats for her own good, getting herself pregnant by accident, but at least Clarice had known what it felt like to marry the man she loved. Evie was starting to believe she was never going to know that feeling.

***

The trouble with Lucas Cain was that he was too handsome. He created a spectacle of himself merely by showing up somewhere. Normally he was used to it, this effect he had on women, but lately he'd taken to wandering the narrow old streets of the

Vieux Carré late in the evening. In the seedier places along Bourbon Street, where the women on the tiny stages wore only a g-string and their obscenely enhanced breasts surpassed the vulgarity of their dancing, in these little hellholes that stank to high heaven, Lucas created quite a stir. Always immaculately groomed in his suit and tie, and never touching alcohol, he confounded the other patrons and even the women on stage. Lucas felt conspicuous for the first time in his life, but it didn't keep him from returning night after night.

It wasn't so much that he liked to watch the dancers, or that he enjoyed the tedious process of watching the women strip out of their skimpy outfits over and over to the pounding rhythms. It was more that he needed the trance they induced to keep him from doing something stupid.

He never failed to cap off an evening with a trip to the men's room, an ancient hole where the smells were particularly rank. Alone in a stall, he lowered his fly and jerked off quickly, the pounding rhythms from the nearby stage egging him on.

This was what he needed to end a perfect evening, to believe that sex was base, that carnal urges were best left to the gutter, that they had nothing to do with love.

***

Late one night, Evie made up her mind. She wasn't going to see Cal Harper anymore. What was the point? She knew she would never marry him. She couldn't even confide in him, there were too many secrets now that she was trying to conceal.

She agreed to meet him one last time in a little place on Chartres Street. They had dinner and then an after dinner drink, and then they said goodbye.

It was a balmy evening in the French Quarter and Evie felt

like walking. She was getting used to being alone. She didn't mind it, really. She walked down Orleans as far as Bourbon Street, but the smells were foul there, so she turned around and walked the other way, heading back to Elysian Fields.

***

In Lucas's dark bedroom, the ceiling fan whirled gently and faint shafts of moonlight came in through the open shutters. He stared blankly at the pattern they made against his wall. The nights were cool enough now that he could lie comfortably under the sheets.

Women are strange creatures, he told himself. They're resilient, tough as nails. They bounce back, they adapt, and yet they can seem so fragile.

Lulled into inattention, he did the unthinkable, he did what he'd swore to himself he wouldn't do. He let his thoughts drift to a memory of Evie, a single memory that he treasured, that shimmered in his mind like a shiny diamond; like the tiny diamond earrings that had glinted in her ears.

It was the night of her father's party, when Lucas had agreed to meet her upstairs, when he'd been out of his mind with lust for her, so much so that he'd agreed to meet her in her room, right under Donovan's nose. It was the night she had sparkled like a precious jewel and it had killed him to watch her out on that dance floor with man after man after man. And there he was, stuck tagging around after Donovan like some trained dog in a tuxedo. Until he couldn't stand it anymore, until he saw his chance to break away and he handed her the glass of champagne.

What a night it was, what an evening for romance. If only he had been free to do exactly as he'd pleased, but it was good enough, meeting her in her room like that. She looked stunning standing there in her open doorway glimmering in the half-light, her hair pulled up and away from her pretty face, showing off her finest features. She looked so much like Clarice it had pained him, only she looked more vivid, more alive.

And she was waiting for him, just for Lucas. Out of all the men at the party who were worth much more than he was, who had impressive educations and long family lines and more than enough diversification to survive a lifetime of financial calamities, he was still the one she was waiting for. And in minutes she'd tugged down the top of that incredible evening gown. Her tits were so pale, so unspeakably white. It was impossible for him to keep his hands off her, to keep his mouth away from those tits. They were too perfectly formed. They hung on her slender chest, two mounds of tender flesh, the nipples tiny and hard. He didn't know how to keep from devouring her.

And when she stripped out of that dress, there she was, in the satin thong and the high-heeled sandals. Her legs looked a million miles long. Her hair pulled up like that, her neck seemed elegant. That's what it was. He didn't think he'd ever seen that before, an elegant neck, with those glinting diamonds winking at him somewhere between those incredible tits and those promising eyes.

This wasn't supposed to happen. His cock was rock hard. He was jerking off, thinking about Evie. It was more than just a single shimmering memory, he remembered every exquisite moment of having his mouth on her, his cock inside her, his arms full of her, and her incredible smell...

His cock was thickening in his fist as he tugged himself vigorously. This was nothing like the quick clandestine erections he forced on himself in the stinking stalls in the strip joints. This was an aching hard-on, a cock that needed to connect.

God, he missed her.

He wasn't supposed to say that. He wasn't supposed to hear his heart shouting out like that. It was supposed to be a done deal. It was work he was after, a stellar career. There was no such thing as love.

And then he thought the most dangerous thought of all, he thought of that tight, tight hole. There it was, the thought that gave it all away. God, he wanted to fuck her.

And before he could stop himself, he was coming all over his hand.

***

Evie slipped into bed naked. It was a perfect night, not too hot, not too cool. She wrapped herself in the blankets and did what she did every night now. It was ingrained in her like a habit. Her fingers were down between her legs.

Tonight she felt unusually responsive; her whole body seemed particularly alive. Within mere moments she was wet. She eased up on her clitoris. She wanted the feeling to linger, this sensation, this lust.

It didn't take much anymore to make her come. A quick visit to the past, the not so distant past that felt like a lifetime ago. She was bending over for Lucas, holding onto the edge of the bed in that tacky motel. His cock was going into her from behind, opening her up and filling her hole.

And it wasn't what he was doing to her that always made her come; it was the sounds she remembered him making, sounds of lust and abandon, sounds that escaped him almost in spite of himself.

That was what made Evie come, the thought that she had once excited him.

Some nights, when she was in the deepest throes of lust, when her fingers were up inside herself and she remembered how compelling it had felt having intercourse with a man at last, the feeling of something pushing up in there, she would think of her parents and how their lust had once filled those rooms. She urged them out of their hiding places, her phantom fucking parents, her fingers working up inside her hole, rubbing that spot, rubbing it and rubbing it until her wrist ached; the spot Lucas had known about, the spot up inside her that his fingers had gone to. She tormented that spot, her hips hiked up high, and she rubbed her clitoris, and together these two actions put Evie into a swoon.

She kept at herself down there, two fingers in her vagina and two fingers on her clit, imagining that the whole house was filled with love, that her parents were still in there somewhere, fucking each other and fucking each other, and maybe even creating her. Maybe that's why she loved this house, this little cottage on Elysian Fields, because it was where she came through, it was where she connected, it was where her spark of life was conceived.

And then she felt like crying when she came.

I'm so lonely, she realized. When is it going to end?

Chapter Twenty-One

More and more frequently, Big Joe found himself working out of the high-rise office tower in New Orleans rather than the office in Solisville. He found this arrangement ensured that Lucas Cain showed up for work with consistency and didn't cancel as many evening meetings. It was an arrangement that secretly thrilled Miss Morrow and, not so secretly, Susie. Any excuse to have Lucas Cain in the office was a perk on par with extra paid vacations.

Big Joe knew in his gut he should let Cain go. He was slacking off and losing focus, but for some reason Big Joe couldn't bring himself to fire him. It was clear even to him that something was coming unglued in Cain. Big Joe was going to try to wait it out. Maybe Cain was his last hope of reconnecting with Evie. If it was, he didn't admit it to himself.

Word had reached him that Evie and Cal Harper were no

longer an item, that Evie had given Cal his walking papers. It didn't surprise Big Joe; he'd been expecting it. All his other carefully thought out plans had fallen to pieces, why not this one? Besides, did it really matter whom Evie married at this point, or if she ever married at all?

Big Joe found himself taking more of his evening meals in the city. The house in Solisville had become like a tomb. Vera was barely speaking to him because he wasn't speaking to Evie, and even though for most of her childhood Evie had been away at school, there was a difference in the kind of emptiness the house embraced now. It was an emptiness that mocked him, that told him even Vera was closer to being a DuMaret than he'd ever be, and that the house belonged more to the hired help than to him.

And more often than not, the evenings at home turned into those long dark nights of the soul, where Clarice's ghost laid down next to him in their old bed and rewound the dream of his life over and over again. It was as if she were trying to make a point. "My baby," she seemed to pleading with him. "Don't forget about my baby, Joe."

When the sun came up, Big Joe would shower and shave and dress for the office while Clarice's ghost stayed stubbornly in that bed, nagging him about Evie. He'd go downstairs and hurry through breakfast, a breakfast where Vera's reproachful face took on the features of Clarice's ghost. But when Big Joe was in the back of the gleaming Lincoln en route to the city, the reverberations of Clarice's voice would at last recede in the distance.

Maybe that was why Big Joe spent more and more time in the city, because Clarice's ghost hadn't thought yet to follow him there.

But there were other ghosts now, ghosts that were just as persistent. Especially Beatrice Amory, his late mother, and she knew the city like the back of her hand. She turned up everywhere. She reproached him for turning his back on her. "I can understand your wanting to take your father's name," she'd say. "I can understand your wanting the recognition. How do you think I felt to have us both cast aside by him? But you shouldn't have turned your back on me, Joe."

Everywhere there were ghosts. They hounded Big Joe. They nipped at his feet. Until one afternoon, to the surprise of everyone, he took off out of the office and went for a long walk.

He headed down river through the French Quarter, then through Faubourg Marigny, where he toyed with the idea of going to see Evie, but instead he kept walking. He wasn't sure what he was trying to prove, but he was on the old stone sidewalks of Bywater before he knew it. It was all still there, street after street of shacks and cramped dwellings squeezed tightly together, the old street names spelled out in tiles embedded in the sidewalks, tiles that had been ancient long before Big Joe was born. Yet for all the things that had stayed the same there was more that had changed.

Affluence had come to town. There had been a rebirth. He knew it had happened because he knew about everything that had to do with local real estate, but it had been decades since he'd actually been home. He barely recognized the house he'd grown up in. It had once been a dilapidated double shotgun shack, but now it was painted in bright Creole colors and upscale renovations were painstakingly underway.

Big Joe stood on the sidewalk and stared at this house that had been his boyhood home, the seat of all his discontent. How did these changes bode for his childhood, for what was past and over? Did this negate those years of poverty? Was this why the ghosts had fled, these bright coats of paint, a hammer and some nails? Had these changes set his demons free?

Big Joe waited but there were no answers, not that he really thought he'd find any. So finally he kept walking. He turned around and headed back the way he had come. And as he drew closer to Elysian Fields, something compelled him to at least stop this time and look at the other old house. By now it was early evening and he was tired. It was too much of an effort to stop himself from ringing her bell, so he went ahead and did it.

When Evie answered the door, she was dumbfounded. "Daddy!" She said it without hesitating, without stopping to think if this was her father or only the man who married her mother.

Big Joe felt encouraged. "Hello, Evie," he said. "Believe it or not, I was in the neighborhood."

***

Everyone, including Lucas, left the office early that day. Big Joe never came back from his walk.

Lucas left his car where it was parked and set out on foot for the Quarter. First he'd have dinner, then get an early start on his usual debauch.

***

Of course, the paint was different, the décor, the furnishings, all different, but there was a feeling, a life to those rooms, that touched Big Joe's heart.

Clarice is here.

He felt it, but it was a different Clarice than the one who haunted him in Solisville. This was the one from happier days, the one he'd first fallen in love with, the Clarice he'd painted the town red with, the woman he'd married.

"It always bothered me," Big Joe confessed, "that I never knew for sure if you were my natural daughter, Evie, but for some reason, I've always been afraid to find out one way or another. I guess I just wanted so much for you to be mine."

Evie didn't know what to say. Her father had never been so candid with her before. She placed his drink in front of him. "I don't know if this is exactly how you like it," she apologized. "Cocktails are a new art for me."

It was bittersweet, the thought that his daughter was trying to cater to him after all the wild days that he'd spent in that very room. They had burned like sparklers those days, crackling, searing, silvery hot. "You look good," he told her. "You look happy."

"I don't know if I'd call it happy," she sighed, "but I'm okay. I love this house. You know, it probably sounds crazy to you, but I feel like this house looks out for me. It takes care of me somehow."

Big Joe drank his drink. He didn't want to talk to her about ghosts. "Have you eaten yet?" he asked. "Let me take you out. There's a place on rue Saint Louis I'd like you to try."

"Really? You want to take me to dinner, daddy? A Harper-free dinner, I hope?"

Big Joe smiled. "Harper-free. I swear."

It took her nearly half an hour to get ready, but when she finally emerged from the bedroom, Big Joe had to look twice. This is Evie, he reminded himself, and the rules have changed. This is a whole new ballgame. Just let it happen.

He opened the door for her and together they walked out to the street. "Evie, I hope you know that Solisville is always going to be your home," he said. "You come out anytime you feel like it, you hear?"

"Okay, daddy," she said. "I will."

She didn't want to talk about Lucas. It seemed like her daddy had won that round fair and square. Having a place of her own, a space to live in, to breathe in, made a world of difference, it seemed. She didn't feel so angry anymore.

"I miss you," he said. "It's not the same."

Evie didn't reply.

Together they walked down Royal Street, and then turned right on rue Saint Louis.

***

The music seemed louder, more monotonous than usual, the girls more desperate, and the dark, putrid room brimmed with hopelessness.

Lucas didn't hang around long. Things seemed changed. He didn't want to be a part of this anymore. He decided it would be best to just call it a night, go find his car and head back home.

It was already after ten o'clock when he walked out onto the street. For a change of pace, he headed down rue Saint Louis.

It was on the sidewalk just outside of Antoine's, with its faux gaslights and the pleated French curtains lining the windows, that he saw the ghosts.

It was Joseph Donovan and Clarice coming out of Antoine's!

Lucas had to look twice.

No, he realized.

"Evie!" he said, calling out to her.

Chapter Twenty-Two

Big Joe was the first to see it, history repeating itself. The thing he'd tried for months to circumvent was happening before his eyes. The ghosts were rising up from rue Saint Louis with slightly new faces, new hearts, new forms, but rising just the same. Just as sure as he and Clarice had risen once, here it was, happening all over again right in front of Antoine's.

"Cain," Big Joe said, "good evening. You remember my daughter Evie." It was killing him to practically hand her over like that. She was as good as gone, Big Joe could tell. My little girl's gone, he thought. But it's good for her to go, Joe. Let her go.

"Lucas!" Evie could barely breathe, but it wasn't because the life was startled out of her, it was because the world itself was rushing in.

"How've you been?" Lucas asked her. "It's been a long time."

"Two months," Evie replied.

"Two months, really?" Lucas would have bet money that it had been longer than that. It had felt like years. For all the nights he'd lain awake, reliving his mistakes, his wretchedness, the emptiness, it should have been years. Two months?

"We were just having dinner," Evie said. "I live here now, you know."

"You do? In the Quarter?"

"Well, almost. I live over on Elysian Fields. In a house that used to belong to my mother."

Lucas felt clumsy. They shouldn't be wasting time, he thought, talking about pointless things like this. They should be kissing, clinging to this good fortune, dragging the river of time for all the empty nights that had been lost. "I don't live too far from here, either," he said. "I have a house in the Lower Garden District. You should come see it some time."

"I'd like that," she said.

Big Joe let it all go. He could feel it leaving, his grasp on everything that he'd tried to hold onto throughout Evie's childhood, but it almost felt good, like a welcome release, as if destiny itself had been waiting for him to get the hell out of the way all these years. Well, maybe this is what Cain needed to snap out of it, whatever the funk was he'd been going through. Maybe the business would get back on track and he could spend more time in Solisville again, less time traveling, keep closer to home.

"You know, it's funny," Evie said. "I had no idea you lived around here. You come visit me, too, okay?"

"I will," Lucas promised.

She fished nervously in her bag for a scrap of paper and a pen. "Here's my number," she said, scribbling it quickly. "Call me anytime." She stole a quick glance at her father, amazed but relieved that he wasn't trying to stop her.

"You look good, Evie," Lucas said, taking the slip of paper from her and sticking it in his pocket. "I'm glad to see it."

"Thanks."

And as if it were natural to choose just that moment for parting, Lucas clasped her hand quickly and then went on his way.

Evie and Big Joe continued on to the old house. They didn't mention Lucas at all. When they'd reached Evie's front door, Big Joe said goodnight. "Hey," he added, "take care of yourself. Don't be a stranger, okay?"

"I won't, daddy. I promise."

She let herself in. She thought she was going to die. Her heart had jumped clear into her throat.

***

When Big Joe's head finally hit the pillow that night in his room up in Solisville, he was alone in the bed. He was sure of it. There would be no ghosts tonight. He was finally going to get some sleep.

***

The following morning, as she always did, Vera woke before dawn. It was her habit to be ready to face the world long before the day help arrived.

As usual, the cook arrived first, followed by Thomas, the chauffeur, who never once ate breakfast at home in all the years he'd been employed by Donovan. The maid arrived last. It was her custom to take her breakfast at home with her family before she headed off to work.

When the help had eaten and the day was underway, the cook prepared Mr. Donovan's breakfast and Vera prepared the table for him in the breakfast room, as she always did.

By seven a.m., Big Joe had yet to emerge. Not a peep had come from the master suite. No footsteps overhead, the shower hadn't run, it was utterly silent.

That's strange, Vera thought. Big Joe was a creature of habit. Even when he wanted to, he could rarely sleep later than six a.m.

By seven-thirty, Vera went to check on him. She knocked first on the outer door, the one that led to the study. When he didn't answer, she went inside and tried the door that led directly to the master bedroom. "Joseph?" she called quietly, but there was no answer. She didn't bother to knock again. She let herself into the room.

It was so peaceful; the room itself seemed at rest. And judging by the serene expression on Big Joe's face, the end had come quietly. He probably hadn't even known.

***

They buried Big Joe Donovan on Evie's twenty-second birthday. She was twenty-two when they lowered her father into the ground and turned over nearly all of Solisville to her, when Donovan & Company became her company, and when the old DuMaret mansion on the river road became Evie Donovan's house.

"I don't know what I'm doing, Vera!" she cried. "How am I supposed to handle this?"

Big Joe's body wasn't even cold in the ground before a long line of lawyers began making their way to Evie. There were papers to read and papers to sign, and Evie tried as hard as she could to grow up overnight.

Once again, the little house on Elysian Fields sat empty, but Evie had no intention of abandoning it. It was just going to have to wait until she could get everything straightened out. In the meantime, she'd moved back into the mansion in Solisville.

What am I going to do with this enormous old cavern, she wondered, this huge creaking thing?

Evie and Vera sorted through Big Joe's personal effects, his clothes, his papers, his mementoes. It was heart wrenching. And it was all the more sorrowful because it made Evie think of Clarice burying her own father, of how she'd had to do these very things while pregnant with Evie, while trying to keep off drugs and booze, while trying to come to terms with a husband who she thought didn't love her.

"It's no wonder…" Evie said quietly.

"No wonder about what?" Vera asked.

"Nothing," Evie sighed. "I just caught a glimpse of why some people are moved to take their own lives."

Vera hugged her. "Don't you talk like that, Evie, we'll get you through this."

Evie had a better appreciation for why her father had tried so hard to marry her off to a family like the Harpers. People like that would have been a Godsend now, but that wasn't how the cards had been dealt. Evie was on her own.

She had Miss Morrow to handle the business end of things. Luckily, Miss Morrow knew as much about the business as anyone. She was tempted to turn the whole thing over to her, but she knew that wasn't what her father had had in mind for his company. In fact, Evie was surprised to learn that there were already documents in place turning the running of the business over to Lucas Cain.

My father really believed in Lucas, she realized, enough to turn everything he'd ever worked for over to him. So why was he so reluctant to let me get anywhere near him if he trusted Lucas enough to take over this empire?

But Lucas Cain was only thirty-five years old. There were bankers and business investors who weren't so happy with this new arrangement. It was an empire, and who was Lucas Cain? Someone who had come from the street. But Big Joe had known better. He knew from his own experience. A man from the street will fight harder because that man has everything to lose.

***

Lucas sat at his breakfast table forcing himself to eat. He needed to keep his head on straight. He needed to stay calm. He could do this. He could handle this. It was what he had worked for his whole life. If this wasn't his destiny, if he were meant to fail, then he wouldn't have made it this far.

It was a good line of reasoning. It helped to keep him on an even keel. Never had he had so many meetings with hostile bankers, men that seemed intent on watching him fail.

But I won't fail, he told himself.

He went upstairs and selected a suit from his closet.

But even Miss Morrow has more formal education than I do…

He stopped himself. He had to be on his own side. If not, all was lost.

***

The well-wishers came out of the woodwork. All of Solisville had attended the funeral. Evie was grateful for the attention, the offers of assistance, the tributes of affection, but at the same time they wore her out.

She realized she didn't really know a quarter of these people. She'd lived her life so remotely, so removed from the whole town. It put her nerves on edge. She saw that she had a certain responsibility to a lot of them. In most cases, she was now their landlord, and she didn't even know where these strangers lived.

Instead of trying so hard to get her married, why hadn't her father spent time showing her what it was he did? She had never felt so overwhelmed or ill equipped for a thing in her life.

Lucas made a trip out to the house to see Evie, but they were both so bewildered by the sudden obligations foisted on them by her father's death that the meeting was by necessity all about business.

"I'm really grateful my father had you, Lucas," she said. "He was counting on you to keep this part of his world alive. He believed in you. I guess you know that."

"Evie, how are you managing?" he replied. He felt like a cad, like there was so much he needed to explain to her, but much of it he didn't even understand himself.

"I'm getting through it. Thank god for Vera. She's been like a mother to me, you know."

He nodded appreciatively. There was so much he wanted to say but the timing was all wrong.

Evie found it curious that she could sit here like this across from him, the man she loved, and not babble on like a fool or feel too overcome with desire to speak. She suddenly saw that there was nothing but time now, nothing urgent, nothing to say that couldn't wait until life resumed its normal course. Yet she couldn't help think how strange it was as she watched Lucas's car pulling out of the drive, that same car she had tried with all her heart to wish into existence on so many lonely nights when she wanted him in her arms. How strange that anything to do with Lucas Cain could wait for another day. What was that telling her about her heart?

Love waits, she realized.

Evie and Vera had managed somehow to clear out all her

father's effects. The master suite no longer contained anything personal. It had once again become a set of rooms. Evie wondered just how many times it had happened over the course of two centuries, how many tears had been shed, hearts broken, loved ones sent off to the hereafter with nothing earthly left but memories. How many times had it happened? And each time, no less painful or bittersweet.

She sat down on the bare mattress and looked around the room. This could be hers now if she wanted it, but she didn't want it. It was too grand a suite for her to ever find comfort in. Besides, she realized with a start, her own mother had died in here. She'd taken her own life and died on this very bed.

She sighed sadly. All those DuMarets, all their trials and triumphs and losses, and she had never known a single one of them. It was their blood in her veins, their lives that had led to hers, but she had to take it on faith that they had ever existed.

Evie decided she would make up the old bed and just leave it as it was. She would have the room closed off and think about it some other day.

In a burst of optimism, she decided to turn the old mattress over before putting on the clean sheets. She flipped it up and tugged it, struggling awkwardly with its bulk, and saw an old letter tucked between the mattress and the old box spring as if it had been purposely hidden away.

Is it a love letter, she wondered, something naughty and risqué? It was usually only the dirty things that got stuck under a mattress.

She pulled the old letter from its envelope and began reading.

My darling, Joe, I have no idea when you're going to find this since I never know when you're coming home anymore. How I wish we could have stayed in Elysian Fields. God we were happy there, weren't we, Joe? But I guess this kind of living suits you best. You always were so impressed by fine things. I wish I could have understood it better right from the beginning. I'm not saying I wouldn't have married you, but maybe I could have at least gone into it with my eyes open, let you marry my money and not take it so personally when you had no time left for me.

Take care of Evie, Joe. You promised me that. Try to keep at least one promise, okay? She's just a baby. She needs you. She's better off with you and Vera than with the mess I make of everything.

I suppose I should apologize for cutting out on you like this, but I don't feel like you're even going to miss me. What happened to us, Joe? Don't tell me it was a scheme from the very start. I'd like to at least pretend you once loved me.

I hate this house, this room, this bed. I wish I could think of somewhere else to die, but then there would be such a scandal, right? And we need to avoid that. DuMarets don't kill themselves, do they? They're made of stronger stuff.

Well, what else can I say? I'm running out of paper. Goodbye, good luck? I love you?

Clarice

PS: Don't forget about Evie. Don't tell her about me, Joe. Give her a break.

Her mother's suicide note, of all things, and that she should find it now.

Evie was grief-stricken all over again. Here it was in black and white, the reason her father had tried so hard to turn Evie into someone else. It all came down to a simple deathbed request, "Don't tell her about me, Joe." It was the only way her father could think of to honor his dead wife, to prove to his wife that he'd loved her, that he could keep a promise.

Well, Vera was right about one thing, these were not the words of a fragile person. This was a woman who decided things for herself. Perhaps that was what was meant by the DuMaret spirit, deciding things for oneself regardless of what everyone else was expecting.

Chapter Twenty-Three

Miss Morrow went in through the connecting vestibule and brought Lucas a cup of coffee. She genuinely missed Mr. Donovan. She'd liked him and she was sad that he was gone, and gone so tragically, but it was like a new world in the office having Lucas Cain in command.

"Anything at all I can help you with, you just buzz me," she assured him again for the millionth time. She set his cup of coffee down in front of him.

Lucas sat behind Donovan's old desk, getting the full view, what it looked like at this end of the power play. "This is a huge office, you know that?" he said. "You must get awfully tired, walking back and forth all day."

"I'm used to it," Miss Morrow replied. And then with a wink, she added, "You'll get used to it, too, Mr. Cain. Don't you worry."

She was a mind reader, that one was. Lucas thanked his lucky stars for Miss Morrow. The women in the office in Solisville weren't nearly as dynamic as she was. "Do you ever go out to the other office?" he asked hopefully. "I could sure use you out there."

Miss Morrow smiled. "I go wherever I'm needed most, which is usually right here."

She wasn't budging. The message was clear – Lucas was on his own. Miss Morrow was something else, a combination drill sergeant, secretary, vice-president and right hand man. She wafted somewhere between the masculine and the feminine, and Lucas didn't think she was married. How would she have found the time? She was always at the office. She was old enough to be Lucas's mother, older than that even, but she wore it well. It was hard for Lucas to think of himself as this woman's boss.

It was hard for Lucas to think of himself as the man in charge of everything. It was funny how long he'd prepared for this day, and when it finally came, it still found him peculiarly unprepared.

He put in longer, harder hours than he ever had before, splitting his time equally between the office in the city and the Solisville concerns. He kept hoping for a free moment to drop in on Evie, to see how she was getting along, but time was a precious commodity at present. He needed more time than he had as it was. He was in need of his own second in command, and that would be a tall order to fill.

Late at night, when he was laying in bed too exhausted to sleep, with dawn just around the corner, he flirted with the notion of stepping down, of giving up the position. It was too much work, this business of being Big Joe Donovan. When had the man ever had time to see his home, his family? There was always too much to do. But when the new day started, Lucas resigned himself to giving it one more try.

He told Miss Morrow to put an ad in the paper. "Find me somebody," he pleaded.

He began to get a better understanding of why Donovan had valued him so highly, and why Donovan had kept him on, even after he'd learned that Lucas had taken his only daughter to some cheap motel. Good help could be very, very hard to find. You started to make concessions.

To help out, Evie had given Lucas a 'gift' in the form of the black Lincoln, and Thomas, Donovan's old chauffeur. She had no more need of them. Rather than sell the car and let Thomas go, the company took over Thomas's employment. Now Lucas could move back and forth in style between the city and Solisville, but it was still a strange feeling looking out his window in the morning and seeing a big black car and man in a black uniform waiting for him to emerge. Lucas wondered how long he would really be able to put up with it. He could see why Evie had wanted to let them go.

Evie. Just the sound of her name these days gave him a sense that it was all going to be okay. What a bitter irony though to be on the verge of re-uniting with her, of having her so close to home, and then all of this, boom, right in their laps.

Maybe that's why Donovan was acting so strangely at the end, Lucas thought now. Maybe on some level he'd already decided he was checking out. How else could anyone explain the way Donovan had acted that last evening, practically pushing Evie on Lucas instead of whisking her away.

Lucas browsed through his appointments, idly wondering when there would be a chunk of time for him to get over and see her, maybe take her to dinner, try to start over. They could go out in public now and do anything they wanted to. There was no reason to worry about gossip. There was no one for the gossip to get back to.

Of course, Lucas was taking it for granted that Evie still wanted to see him. That night in front of Antoine's she'd looked willing enough.

But how was he supposed to explain to her why he'd chosen to stop seeing her the way he had? And how was he going to rationalize it to himself? Just because he'd taken over Donovan & Company didn't make him immune to the capricious whims of love.

He was finished in the city for the day. He told Miss Morrow to call down for Thomas, that he was ready to head out to the Solisville office.

***

These days the old house was almost unbearably quiet. Evie had let the cook and the maid go, too. It was just Vera and her now.

She wandered the old rooms noticing everything as if she had just come to live there. She saw the house now in terms of the DuMarets, their rich history, their long reign on the mighty Mississippi when cotton was king.

How could I have lived this long and never really felt this house? It has a life of its own.

She remembered Lucas's shock the night she'd confessed to feeling trapped, an awful house, she'd called it. Now she understood a little better why he had been shocked. Terrible things might have happened there, when you counted the tragic lives of each individual slave, and not just the more recent tragedies of Evie's grandfather or of Big Joe and

Clarice. Still, it was all part of a larger history. It was a testament to the overall pageantry of life.

Evie could see that now. All of her family, including her, were tiny pieces of the larger mosaic that made up Louisiana's heritage.

What was I running from? Maybe just her father, she was running from her father. But what was more important was who she was running to, a truer idea of herself. And that had come in part from discovering Clarice, with all her strengths and imperfections.

Evie felt proud of the house now, and she wished she'd understood all of it better while her father had still been alive. What it must have meant to him to rise up from such lowly beginnings and take a seat at the head of the table of such a fine old home.

I took so much for granted, she scolded herself, but then how was I to know? Everyone was so intent on leaving me in the dark.

She spent occasional nights sitting up late in her father's room, that grand master bedroom where so much life had come and gone… babies born, old men dying, fever epidemics coming to claim the weak and, of course, a telltale suicide every now and then. All of those human markers had visited that single room. And for how many nights over the course of twenty-two years had her father laid his head on that pillow, dreaming his own dream of life until the final curtain fell? It seemed a shame, really, to keep it closed up.

One morning, when she woke early, the sun streaming through the slats in the blinds and all of it diffusing through the mosquito netting draped around her, Evie had an epiphany. She wanted to give up the old house and all its land and turn it into a museum. Let people come from all walks of life and see for themselves the place that had once been home to such a long line of proud and irascible people called the DuMarets. It was triumphs like theirs, and tragedies, and some unspeakable acts of brutal human degradation that made the land of Louisiana the colorful and complex land it was today. Hers was one of the few plantation homes still owned by an individual, most had been turned over to historical preservation societies long ago.

It was hard for Evie to bring herself to tell Vera about her decision. The house had been Vera's home for over forty years, but strangely enough, when Vera finally got the news, she was proud of Evie, and proud of having been part of the final legacy of the DuMarets.

"Your family would have approved wholeheartedly," she said. "And your mother would have been proud. It's very generous of you, Evie, to give your wealth out to the people this way."

Evie hadn't thought of it like that, but if what she was doing was going to give something back to the people – people she had barely acknowledged during the early course of her life – then it was okay with her.

It turned out Vera had been feeling a little restless anyway. The house was too big, and with just her and Evie and no one to help Vera keep it clean, it was becoming too much for a woman of sixty-seven to handle. So Evie decided to buy Vera a home in town, a smaller and much more manageable house with its own unique history and charm.

When the various papers were signed and the announcements were made, on the evening before the packing would begin, Evie wanted to be alone again, out there in the night, and celebrate this victory on her own.

In honor of her mother, she took a bottle of vintage champagne with her to help her celebrate. With her bottle in tow and the stars up above her, she wandered all over the perfectly manicured lawns remembering every Donovan gala and the spot where she and Lucas had made love outside the gazebo.

She wondered now how many other lovers might have met there over the course of the centuries. Surely she hadn't been the only one to succumb to so much lust and the urge to feel alive.

She worked her way carefully through the overgrown tangle of trees and found her old rock. She hadn't been out there in months, certainly not since before her father died, and not since the nights of Lucas Cain.

Lucas. Just the thought of his name pierced her heart. She was going to have to get over to the offices of Donovan & Company one of these days and pay him a visit to give him a piece of her mind.

She leaned against her rock and drank her champagne from the bottle. It felt good, she realized, turning over the house to strangers. It was a relief and a release, and she was looking forward to returning to the house on Elysian Fields and being done with it. She tried to picture what it was going to be like... long lines of ticket holders filing through the mansion's old rooms. "Here is where Clarice DuMaret Donovan, the noted beauty of the French Quarter, killed herself. And here, ladies and gentlemen, is where her husband, Big Joe, born Joseph Amory of Bywater, suffered his fatal heart attack, letting history repeat itself to the fullest with this final ironic twist. And out here on these breathtaking grounds, if you'll look very closely ladies and gentlemen, amid these ancient old oak trees dripping with Spanish moss, under the blessings of a watchful heaven, you'll see the very rock where Evie Donovan disgraced herself, behaving like a wanton little fool for one Lucas Cain, unloading her dreaded virginity at last." There would be 'oohs' and 'aahs' and general astonishment all around. Evie almost wished she could be there to see it.

Drinking a final toast to the vast impressive property, she took her champagne and wandered back toward the house. On the porch swing she planted herself, intent on drinking every last drop from the bottle. She was already feeling drunk; it was not a feeling she was accustomed to.

At the other end of the veranda, leaning against the old railing, Evie saw her father smoking a cigarette in the dark. She watched him curiously. He didn't seem to know that he wasn't supposed to be there. Maybe he was lost, but he seemed so content that she didn't want to disturb him. He didn't seem to notice she was there.

And then she realized that someone she didn't recognize at all was sharing the porch swing with her.

It was an old woman in an old-fashioned nightcap and gown. She had a stern expression on her face and she rocked the swing slowly.

A DuMaret matriarch, no doubt, thought Evie.

Gradually, as she looked around her, she noticed for the first time in her life that the entire yard was alive with people. None of them seemed aware that the others were right there beside them, moving from place to place in the dark. Some seemed on a determined mission, while others appeared to be content to stroll aimlessly.

There were DuMarets mixed in with hundreds of slaves, and Evie watched it all from the vantage point of the old porch swing.

The greatest moment of all was when a young woman made her way through the crowd and ran up the porch steps. She was vibrant and beautiful, even in the dark. She wore a shimmering wisp of a dress, as if maybe she'd been out dancing, and she seemed breathless, in a hurry to catch life. She came right over to Evie and smiled a winning, vivacious smile. She was the only one of the whole crowd who seemed to know that Evie was there.

"Mommy?" Evie asked hopefully.

Mommy, the woman nodded in reply.

When Evie woke, Vera was standing over her, shaking her gently. She said, "Honey, wouldn't you be more comfortable sleeping in your own bed?"

Chapter Twenty-Four

The house on Elysian Fields welcomed Evie with an aura of serenity and good cheer. She was convinced that human happiness had triumphed within those walls and she was hoping to keep it that way.

It was a much better approach to life, four-and-a-half contained rooms. It helped Evie feel like she was in control of where her destiny was taking her.

She learned to cook and she kept the little house spotlessly clean. And she got out more. She went on daily excursions investigating the Quarter. She even walked the quaint streets of Bywater, imagining how it had looked in the days of her father's childhood, and wondering where it was that Lucas Cain had called home.

Once she even ventured as far as the old Business District and investigated the city headquarters of Donovan & Company, the high-rise office tower she now owned.

Her secret motivation had been to run into Lucas Cain, but she soon learned from the efficient Miss Morrow that Lucas was now spending most of his time out in the Solisville offices. In fact, he practically lived there now. Miss Morrow was sure Lucas's house in the Garden District was up for sale.

Lucas had quickly fallen into what had been Evie's father's routine. How ironic that she was in the city now and he was up in Solisville. "He seems to be managing things well, then?" Evie inquired.

Miss Morrow replied with a whole-hearted "Yes!" and there was a gleam in her eye that set Evie's nerves a little on edge. She realized she was jealous of Miss Morrow, of her close proximity to Lucas.

"Well, I'm glad to hear it," Evie said, putting her best face on the envy she was feeling. "I know he worked hard for it. It was what he wanted above everything." She didn't go so far as to say he wanted it more than he wanted me, but she felt it acutely just the same.

The office seemed to be less than approving of Evie's presence, so she didn't go back there again. She knew she was only in the way. She owned the structure, she owned the name, but the work that got done there took care of itself like a well-oiled machine and didn't require the presence of an actual Donovan to keep it raking in money.

***

Lucas had ultimately held his own with the long, grim parade of bankers and investors that had descended on him after Donovan's funeral, and his reward for surviving the tedium of it was that he was now officially hopelessly overworked. But he was adapting to the things that were required to be efficient at the helm of Donovan & Company.

He didn't especially enjoy living in Solisville. It was a quaint town with a colorful history, but Lucas hardly had time for quaintness and history. It was with reluctance that that he'd put his house in the city up for sale, but it wasn't as if it held any treasured memories for him or even possessed much in the way of atmosphere. He had hardly spent much time there since he first bought it. Basically, it was where he'd showered and slept. He'd never once entertained in the house, and for all he knew his hired cleaning service felt more at home there than he did.

He knew that Evie and Vera had both left the DuMaret mansion and it made Lucas feel a little sad, but he thought that Evie had made an admirable decision. The whole town was buzzing with the news.

One afternoon, he asked Thomas to drive him past the old place. It was poignant. There was a full scale restoration underway. The house was crawling with workmen and other strangers carrying clipboards and looking harried. His dreams of eventually being a frequent guest at the old DuMaret dining room table never came to pass, but he didn't really mind. Look what it had gotten Donovan, a wife who had killed herself and a daughter who had caused him to lose an awful lot of sleep.

Evie... What was he going to do about her? There was so much unfinished business there. If he let it go too long, there wouldn't be any point in trying to fix the situation. She would surely be on to someone new by then. So why was he dragging his feet? What was he so afraid of? He could at last have the world on a string now, just like Donovan and Clarice had had when Lucas idolized them as a boy. He could have the world now, and love, too. Why was he being so stubborn?

Because look what happened to Donovan and Clarice, he warned himself.

But I'm not Donovan and Evie is in a class by herself.

***

Evie spent her days decorating the little cottage with treasures she'd find on her excursions into the world of the Vieux Carré, and her evenings were usually spent alone with a cocktail in the secrecy of her little courtyard tucked inside the walls of the jungle garden. But the nights on Elysian Fields were still haunting, and it wasn't her parents' ghosts that filled her dreams anymore, it was Lucas.

Why did she have to be so immature? Why couldn't she just let go of him, once and for all? Why couldn't she face the fact that her father had been right and it had only been a brief, if momentous, affair? Other women had affairs and it didn't bring their worlds crashing down around them. Evie knew that if she could come to terms with this, she could let Lucas go for good. Maybe she would even grow up.

She lay awake in bed. The clock in the front parlor declared daintily that it was four a.m.

Why did it always come down to this, her lying alone in bed and staring at four walls?

***

Lucas turned out the bedside light and his weary head hit the welcome pillow. He had just come from another long, tedious dinner party in a potential client's home where, try as he might to keep the conversation focused on the business at hand, the client's wife, with the aid of too much Pouilly-FuissÈ, monopolized Lucas's attention by flirting shamelessly right in front of her pathetic husband. This particular minx had gone so far as to corner Lucas out on the patio, slip an arm familiarly around his waist, and then none too discreetly slide her hand down to his ass and help herself to a good handful of it.

He lay as a dead weight in the dark, his eyes closing, and in a matter of moments he'd be gone to the next world… but there it was. He groaned in exhaustion. How could it be that every fiber of his being could be nearing a coma, but his cock could still spring up with a will all its own?

***

Evie had long ago given up any pretenses of falling back to sleep. She knew what her body was craving, and it was best to just go ahead and give in.

Her nightgown was shoved up over her tits and her panties were down around her knees. With the blankets kicked back, she was deep in a world of lust, oblivious to everything but the sordid things she was doing for Lucas in her head.

Her clitoris was very accommodating, sensitive and responsive to the slightest touch. It didn't take much coaxing from her fingers to fuel the dirty pictures in her head.

Her mind was undecided about whether she and Lucas were naked outdoors after dark or back in that crummy motel. Sometimes they were inside, sometimes they were out, but the thing that remained constant was that she was naked and on all fours for him, taking his hard cock all the way up inside her. It was what she preferred, bending over for him, surrendering the goods completely, letting him have his way with her, wondering what he might make her do next.

Her fingers tugged her nipple now and egged the pictures on.

***

Miraculously, Lucas was wide awake. It didn't matter if it was four in the morning. When it came to servicing his demanding dick, even sheer exhaustion took a back seat. It was curious how a body so depleted of energy could sustain such a killer hard-on. His cock felt wired, it felt full of raw nerve endings, it made even the slightest pressure of his fist get him even harder.

He was thinking about Evie again, of course. He couldn't go more than a night without putting her through her paces, her lovely, lovely paces.

Usually all it took for him to come was to think about her on her hands and knees for him, her pretty mouth opening around his shaft, taking him all the way in, but tonight, his imagination felt fertile. She was assuming all his favorite positions, and he wasn't near to coming yet; he was only getting more and more aroused.

***

They were outside now, they were definitely outside. They were underneath that weeping willow where Evie had gone briefly once with Cal. She and Lucas were safely hidden from the world even though it was broad daylight. She could see everything. Her dress was hiked up around her waist and her legs were spread wide. Lucas was doing that thing he did with his fingers. They were stuck up inside her and rubbing her like crazy. She was shaved down there again and spread so wide that she could readily see it all, every wrinkle and fold of her pussy, and Lucas's fingers stuck up in her hole. She wondered now what that would really look like, Lucas's fingers, or anything for that matter, stuck up inside her hole.

She applied more pressure to her clitoris thinking maybe she would shave again. That had seemed to get Lucas very turned on.

***

Evie was bending over for him, clear over like she'd done that time in the motel, holding onto her ankles, giving it all up. She was open wide, everything unbelievably exposed. Her pink lips were slick and fat, engorged, and at the very center of her that tight little hole was pushing open, that tight little hole that was somehow going to stretch enough to accommodate his aching cock. It was right there again, in front of his mind's eye.

In real life he hadn't been able to resist it. He'd sunk his face right up in there between her legs, going for her clitoris relentlessly, smothering himself in her soaking pussy. She had come quickly then, a guttural cry rising out of her while she shoved her pussy down harder on his face. But this time he wanted his cock inside her. He wanted to fuck her in this very unlikely, unflattering position. That hole was going to open wide for him and he was going to fuck the hell out of her.

***

Evie couldn't hold back the orgasm any longer, and she didn't want to. She wanted the release. She tugged furiously on her nipple now and rubbed her clit faster. She was bringing it on at last. Her body spasmed with the intensity of the climax, the hot thrill burning through her veins in waves.

She was thinking of something new when it happened. She was in the back seat of the black Lincoln. She was dressed to the nines in a black evening gown. She wasn't wearing her panties. Lucas was in that incredible tuxedo, his zipper down and his thick cock out. They were both facing forward and she was planted on his lap. She had her billowy skirts raised high and her thighs spread wide, so that anyone could see that Lucas's cock was stuffed up her hole.

He was fucking her, he was fucking Evie, and Thomas was right there, he was in the front seat, as always, but it was like he didn't care or maybe like he approved. And they were down there in the Quarter, their big fat Lincoln taking up the whole street.

Anyone could see, any poor fool passing by could see right into the back seat of the Lincoln and see plainly that Lucas was fucking her, that it was okay finally for these two beautiful people to be out in the open and in love.

***

Lucas shot his come in hot spurts all over his hard stomach. And as always as he came there was a feeling of emptiness careening wildly through the ragged chambers of his heart, as if his chest had become a wide open hole, void of anything, certainly void of love.

He couldn't go on like this. It was crazy. He knew he wanted to see her again. He was going to have to bite the bullet and call Evie. He had to get all his cards out on the table and find out once and for all if she was willing to forgive him and start again.

He made his way into the bathroom to clean up, but he kept the lights off. He didn't want to see the look on his face. He was disgusted with himself, for the things he'd let slide in life in pursuit of his career.

He made his way back to his bed, and this time when his head hit the pillow his mind was brimming with pictures of Evie, of how he had her in his dreams, her arms around him, her legs parted, his cock going in, but most of all her heart open, a place in her world that had his name on it in permanent ink. She wanted her to promise him that she wasn't going to leave him no matter how many times the devil might tempt her with something better, like a Mr. Caster from Savannah.

Chapter Twenty-Five

The next day the phone in the front parlor rang and Evie answered it. "Hello?" she said.

Lucas forced himself to speak. "Evie, how are you?"

Lucas.

"I'm in from Solisville and I was wondering... I know it's a little last minute, but do you want to get together?"

There it was, Evie thought, back again, that inimitable thrill in her belly. "Lucas, I would love that."

"I can come get you," he offered. "Thomas is getting the night off and I've got my own car. I'd really like to see you."

"Why don't you just come here?"

He hadn't wanted to say it, but that was exactly what he'd wanted to hear. He wanted to be alone with her, some place private.

They arranged to get together at seven.

By six forty-five, Evie's heart was back in her throat as it had been that fateful evening outside of Antoine's. What a detour that had turned out to be, going to sleep on cloud nine, thinking that things with Lucas and her father were finally going to be okay, and then the following morning the whole house of cards tumbling down and her father was dead.

Lucas arrived punctually at seven. When she opened the door for him, it nearly broke her heart. He looked as handsome as ever in his suit and tie. He looked a little tired, and maybe that had aged him, but in her opinion the age suited him.

"Evie, it's so good to see you," he said, looking larger than life on her little porch. "It's been ages." He thought she looked happy, a woman at peace with life.

"It hasn't really been that long. You were out to the house after my father died."

"I'm not counting that. I was talking about September. That's when I last saw you. That's how it feels anyway."

She brought him inside.

The infamous day at the motel, she realized, that's when time had stopped for him, too.

Lucas followed her out back to her secluded little courtyard, the world where Evie spent so many of her private hours.

"Is this your first time back in a while?" she asked.

"Yes," he said, sitting down awkwardly on one of her ancient cast iron chairs. "And I've sold my house. I was never there anymore. Piece by piece I had managed to move everything to Solisville."

"Well, if you ever need a place to stay in the Quarter, you're always welcome to stay here. I have another little bedroom upstairs."

Lucas was pleasantly taken aback. "Frankly, it would never

have occurred to me. Thank you, Evie. Under the circumstances, that's very generous of you."

"What circumstances? You mean my father? I'm not really in mourning anymore. I've gotten on with my life."

"No, Evie," he said, stumbling over his words, "that wasn't what I meant. I meant me, how I've treated you. It's a very generous gesture on your part. I know I left you hanging. It wasn't very kind of me."

Evie wasn't sure what to say. She let his words float on the air. It was true enough, even though her heart had always told her Lucas was going to come back to her, he had waited until he no longer had to choose between her and her father to do it. What did that say about him? Was she sure she wanted to know? "Well, just the same, you're welcome to stay in my house whenever you want to. Can I ask you something? It might seem a little abrupt."

"You can ask me anything, Evie."

"Why did you want to see me tonight?"

"I missed you," he confessed, "and I wanted to explain."

"Explain why you chose a job with my father over being with me?"

Lucas stared at her uncomfortably. "Yes, I guess that's it in a nutshell."

"That night we ran into each other outside of Antoine's, were you really going to call me? Were you really going to invite me over to your house? You can be honest, you know. You've got your job now."

"Yes, I've got my job now."

"So we can both be honest."

This was his chance to come clean with her, he knew it, but he felt too on the spot. He wanted to get the hell out of there and, like some scared little kid, just run away. "Evie, I wanted to keep seeing you from the beginning," he tried to explain, "but as much as I didn't want to hurt you, I didn't want to get hurt, either."

"I know the job meant a lot to you. You didn't want to lose it."

"I'm not talking about the job. I was ready to give up the job. It was your father who wanted me to keep it. He begged me to keep the job and give you up, to give you a chance at long-term happiness, he said, a thing he didn't think you could have with a man like me. I went home that day and I gave it some thought, and I felt I had to agree with him. There are probably men out there much better suited to your happiness in the long run."

Evie was beside herself. "What is that supposed to mean, that my happiness is a thing decided by others, without my input, in a meeting behind closed doors?"

"Evie, please, that's not what I meant."

"And why is it okay now to see me? What's so different about my long-term happiness now? What changed your mind?"

"I don't blame you for being angry, Evie, I don't. I wish I could explain it to you in simple words."

"Use any words you like, Lucas, I'm all ears."

"You frightened me, okay?" he blurted clumsily.

Evie was skeptical. She thought of herself naked and bending over for him in the dark woods, her mind in a swoon of confusion, her virginity surrendered up to him one slow, painful inch at a time.

"I frightened you?"

"Yes, you did, and your money did, too, okay? We come from different worlds, Evie. You're still young. You don't know what all this money can mean, what's going to be expected of you."

"Don't underestimate me anymore, Lucas, I have a good idea."

He was silent. He should shut up before he made himself sound even more of a fool.

"Look, I know about my father," she said. "I know that what you tried to tell me about him, well, I know it was true, I know that now. And I know about my mother, too. I have a feeling you knew more about her than you were willing to let on, but I also see a different side of it. I think my father really loved my mother. It doesn't mean he didn't make mistakes, but it wasn't just money, Lucas. And I'm not just money, either." She felt desperate.

"I know you're not."

"I'm not just money…" she choked on a sob. "I'm a human being!"

"Evie…"

"I'm sorry, but I'm just so sick of it. Why did you leave me, Lucas? I waited so long for you to come back for me." But she wasn't going to let herself get hysterical. That wasn't what she was about anymore. The funeral was her hysteria and now it was over. She had to pull herself together. "Lucas, would you mind?"

"What?"

"Can we go inside and start again? I haven't even offered you a drink."

***

Over her little refrigerator, Evie had accumulated quite a well stocked bar. "I made dinner, too," she told him. "I don't know if you're hungry, but it's here. I can cook now, you know. I'm practically normal. All that money hasn't been as much of a stumbling block as you might think."

"Evie, I'm sorry about that. It came out all wrong."

"That's okay," she said smiling. "I'm not insulted."

Lucas watched her at work in her tiny kitchen. She seemed

more at home here than she ever seemed in Solisville, and there was something else, too; she seemed to have grown up.

Evie liked the way her little kitchen looked with Lucas standing in it, but she knew better than to tell him a thing like that. She didn't want to scare him away. She made a mental note to herself that tonight was all about not scaring him away.

She fixed him a gin and tonic and a poured a cognac for herself. She needed something serious to calm her nerves. "Here," she said, handing him his drink. "Cheers."

"Cheers, Evie." He pulled out a kitchen chair and sat down.

"We don't have to sit in here if you'd rather sit somewhere more comfortable. I mean, I do have three-and-a-half other rooms to choose from."

"I'm fine here, Evie, it's okay. It's a great little house. I like it. But if you don't mind?"

"I don't mind."

He took off his suit jacket and loosened his tie. "It's been a long day," he said. "And I had a late night last night."

She sat in the chair next to him. It felt perfect, being with Lucas in her tiny kitchen. She was afraid to spoil the mood by talking. She never knew what was likely to come out of her mouth these days. She didn't spend too much time around people.

"Cheers," he said again, chiming his glass with hers.

"Cheers," she echoed. The liquor was smooth and warm. It burned slightly going down her throat. The aroma immediately brought to mind a lifetime of unexpected memories. From now on, she realized, cognac would always remind her of her father.

She felt an ache inside. It happened every time she remembered that she was alone now, that he was gone.

"You look sad," Lucas observed.

"I was thinking about my father. I'm glad he and I had a chance to make up before he died. That dinner we had together at Antoine's was probably the most enjoyable time I'd had with him in my life. It felt like the first time he was really with me, you know? Most of the time it seemed like he was always thinking about work, or something that took his thoughts a million miles away. But that night at Antoine's he was right there. It was where he met my mother, you know? He met her in front of Antoine's."

"I didn't know that," Lucas admitted.

"Really? You know, I'd started to think there wasn't anything you didn't know about my parents. Maybe I was getting a little paranoid?"

"A little. There's a lot I didn't know about your parents. I was just a kid, Evie, a very impressionable kid."

"And what would you say made the most profound impression on you in terms of my parents?"

A sly smile took over his face. He hadn't prepared for a question like that. "I don't think I'd better say," he replied.

"Oh no," she protested. "Now you have to say. What is that look for? I need to know."

"I saw your mom naked once. It was quite profound."

Evie's eyes widened. It was the last thing she'd expected him to say. She found it utterly endearing. "You saw my mom naked?"

"Yes."

"Did she know you could see her?"

"Oh yeah, she knew, but she was a little tipsy."

Evie laughed. "Well, come on, tell me. What did she look like?"

Lucas couldn't believe he was telling her this. Until this moment, he'd regarded it as shameful, that he could have been so sexually obsessed with Clarice, and then have made love to her daughter, yet now it seemed like a simple thing.

I can do this, he thought, I can say it. They're just words, words describing a memory of something beautiful that touched me a long time ago.

"She looked just like you," he admitted. "Her body was very beautiful, very erotic looking. I used to have fantasies about her. I wanted to have sex with her, Evie, she was so full of life." And as he spoke, he could feel Clarice's hold on his heart fading, as if the sound of his words in the room had broken a secret spell. Finally, her let her go forever. It happened as easily as that.

Evie said, "I'm flattered, Lucas. You're so lucky. I would have loved to have known my mother. I think she was something special."

"She was special, Evie, but she was troubled, too. She had demons."

She thought she knew those demons well. There were millions of them in her family, each with a little dollar sign attached to it.

"You remind me of her in a good way,' he went on. 'You're a happier version, more content. You're not running from your life, you're living it."

Evie knew she had her father to thank for that, in his convoluted way. He had kept her a blank canvas. He had given her the gift of her own destiny, untainted by her mother's missteps. Because of a promise he had kept, Evie had grown up free the way her mother had wanted her to.

Lucas set his glass down on the table. "I admire you, Evie, you know that? I spent my whole life running from myself."

"What did you have to run from? Lucas, you're perfect."

"I'm hardly perfect. Jesus, Evie, I'm a mess. I'm always running from this feeling that I never should have been born."

She was incredulous. "Are you crazy? How can you say that? You're the only thing about life that's really exciting. How can you think you shouldn't have been born? Then where would I be? Bored beyond belief that's where, and still a virgin, too. I hope you're not forgetting that?"

Lucas looked into those eyes, bright blue and eager. How did she always manage to seem so unaffected by the ugliness of life? "You're sweet," he said, and he leaned over the table and kissed her. "And to answer your question, I'm not forgetting. How could I?" He took her glass from her and set it down. "Come here," he said, scooting his chair out.

She got out of her own chair and went and sat on his lap. It was as if nothing had ever come between them.

"There are things I should explain," he tried to begin.

"Don't," she said. "Not now." She kissed him full on the mouth, like she'd been dreaming about for months. I'm not letting him go this time, she told herself. "I don't need to know, Lucas. I really don't. What I need is to be with you, to make love, right now."

***

He eased her down on the bed, smoothing her hair out of her face. She was so pretty, and she was in his arms again. How could he have thought for a minute that there was anything less than her in the dream of his life? The gutter was where his mother was content to try to put the pieces together, but that was his mother's choice. Lucas had always chosen something more.

He unbuttoned the delicate white buttons down the front of her shirt. She was already breathing heavily. Life excited this girl something fierce. "You like sex, don't you, Evie?" he asked quietly.

She smiled. "I missed you so much," she replied. She pulled open her shirt for him. She was wearing a lace bra, petal pink that clasped in front. She undid the clasp, and he did the rest, pushing the bra open, bringing her tits out.

He couldn't help himself, he would eat her alive. It felt like forever since he'd seen those tits. Why did they always have to be so white? Why did the nipples have to sit just so, tiny and hard on the tips of those perfect, fleshy mounds? His mouth was all over her, devouring her again.

Evie gasped from the sudden intensity of it. His mouth on her nipple always felt so good. It made her want to spread her legs for him. It made her burn down there. It made her whole pussy come alive.

She was in a hurry to feel him, to feel it all, his mouth on her between her legs, his cock inside her, everything. It had been too long, too many nights alone. She couldn't hold back the tidal wave of lust this time. It was stronger than she could manage. She felt engulfed by it. She tugged down the zipper on her skirt.

Lucas backed away. She seemed to be in a real heat. He unbuttoned his shirt quickly and then he was out of his trousers. He helped her pull her skirt down and off. "You don't play fair, do you?" he teased, getting a load of the prettiest pair of stockings he'd ever seen. They shimmered; they hugged the tops of her slender thighs with a captivating network of pale pink lace. Her mound was sheathed in a simple provocative strip of satin the color of skin. It had the effect of utter nudity, smooth, hairless nudity. He couldn't wait, he couldn't resist. He knew what was hiding under that strip of smooth satin – skin, flesh, nothing but flesh, delicate, tender, and soaking.

He pulled the fabric aside and there it was, just like he'd remembered it, the swelling lips pouting tauntingly on her perfectly hairless mound. He knew she was wet, he could smell her from here.

Evie parted her legs for him as he fell to his knees. His mouth was on her in a heartbeat. She caught her breath it felt so incredible. His tongue went right to it, to the tip of her clitoris, just under the sensitive hood of it, licking like mad. Oh God, she thought, I'm going come in two seconds. She pulled determinedly on her tits, working the stiff nipples between her fingers. "Oh God, Lucas," she moaned. "I'm coming!"

He didn't doubt it, he felt like coming himself, his rock hard cock stuffed uncomfortably in his briefs. He pulled open her slippery lips, keeping her clit completely exposed, and went at it feverishly with his tongue. Pulling the hood back now, sucking the clit itself between his lips, he tortured that swollen engorged nub with his merciless tongue.

She let out an anxious, guttural sort of sound. "God!" she gasped.

He slid two fingers up her unsuspecting, soaking hole and she clamped down tight and hard, her thighs hugging his head.

"Oh no," she cried, "I'm coming... I'm coming..."

He moved those fingers inside her urgently, fighting the tightness that was squeezing him hard. His nose was pressed deep in her mound, her scent drowning him now as he kept her clit hostage.

"Oh God, oh...!" she wailed, and went to the next level. She opened her legs now and held her thighs wide. "God, yes," she gasped, encouraging him, still coming, baring down rhythmically on his fingers and jerking hard against his tongue. Her ecstasy exploded in tiny gasping cries. "Stop," she begged him now, thoroughly exhausted, the wave receding. "Stop, please." Everything was suddenly too sensitive.

Lucas stood up and smiled at her, his cock bulging inside his briefs. "Well, that was a nice surprise."

Evie was still too breathless to speak. She nodded her agreement instead.

"Do you want a minute to catch your breath?" he asked.

She shook her head. She got herself onto her knees, and then yanked his briefs down his thighs. His cock sprang out thick and hard. Her gorgeous ass in the air, the thong cutting a perfect line between her fleshy cheeks, she leaned down and took his cock in her mouth. She stretched her lips around it, sucking it up and down, her lips pulling at the uncircumcised flesh as his cock slid in and out over her tongue.

He picked up his rhythm then and fucked her mouth hard. She had to hold onto him in order not to fall off the bed. She gave over completely to his rhythm, trying not to choke, trying to let him ride her, the spit collecting in her mouth and easing the friction, helping the thick intrusion slide. She worked it until her jaw ached.

"Evie," he gasped quietly. "Oh, sweetie…" He didn't want to come like this. He didn't know if he had it in him tonight to come more than once. He begged off.

She got up off the bed and stripped out of her soaking thong.

Once again she created for him a memory to last a lifetime in those shimmering pink stockings topped with lace, a pair of high heels and nothing else. "I don't think I'll ever get tired of looking at you," he confessed.

"I hope you never do."

He pulled his briefs all the way off and sat down on the bed, his cock still ready, aching, swollen, anticipating the thrill of what was still to come. He was going to put on a condom.

"You don't have to," she said. "I'm prepared. I'd been hoping this was going to happen."

He smiled. "Come here," he said. "Sit here."

She was delighted to accommodate him. She kicked off her shoes and climbed on the bed, lowering herself onto his lap. It had been months since she'd last had intercourse. She felt incredibly tight. Her hole stretched uncomfortably at first, but then she pushed herself all the way down on him.

They gasped in unison as they collided, his cock moving all the way up as her vagina opened to receive it.

He held her there in his lap, his hands full of her fleshy ass. He rocked her on him slowly, feeling the full depths of that incredibly tight passage.

Her arms around his neck, she clung to him, letting him rock her, letting him probe up into her, stretching her open slowly, rhythmically, until she was thoroughly planted on his lap.

He laid back on the bed then, his hands still gripping her ass as she sat on him, and he helped her ride him, he helped her ease her hole up and down along the length of his cock. It was such a snug fit, he felt delirious. Her hole hugged the skin along the length of his shaft and massaged it up and down, up and down, pulling the skin to the head of his cock, pushing it back down again, the swollen head exposed when it poked clear up into her. What a tight hole, he thought, what a wonderfully tight, impossible little hole she has.

The view he had of her was also incredible. Her legs parted as she impaled herself, her smooth shaved lips opening wide, revealing it all. He watched his cock emerge from her, slick with her wet arousal as she rose up over him, the flesh of her tits bouncing gently with every trip she took back down.

Evie's legs ached. She couldn't keep this up much longer, and as if he were reading her mind, he pulled her down on top of him. He kissed her, and then spilled her over onto her back.

They uncoupled, and he spread himself over her. "Evie," he

said, "I want to sleep here with you tonight. I don't want to go."

She had hoped they would at least have sex, but she hadn't expected to get this lucky. "Okay," she said.

"You're sure you want me to stay?"

"I'm very sure."

It was a far cry from his lonely nights on Bourbon Street. Lucas couldn't have been happier. "I'll stay, on one condition," he teased her.

"And what's that?"

"You know what that is. You've got to give it up the way I like it."

***

Naked, sweating, every muscle straining, they were at each other again. They couldn't stop.

A single lamp burned low on the table beside the bed. It had gotten quite late. Lucas had Evie where he wanted her now, her knees planted far apart on the bed, her ass arched up high, and everything about her pussy on complete display for him. His cock could get in there deep. In this position he had unhindered access to her hole. He could watch the hole stretch to take him in, watch his shaft pull back out. Go in again and come back out…

And all the while the hole hugged him and Evie made the most entrancing sounds, deep groans peppered with little cries that were muffled in her pillow.

She braced herself for his increased speed. She waited in anticipation of his force. It was what she liked best, knowing when he was about to come, hearing it in his voice, feeling it in his loins as they slammed against her backside.

And there it was, she felt it, her fingers clutching at the mattress. He was just about to come. He really let loose on her then

She bit down on her pillow to keep her cries from filling the whole house.

Lucas gripped her hips tight, pummeling into her, his cock swelling up a final time as it exploded. He cried out when he came it felt so intense.

Evie was whimpering underneath him as she arched the small of her back up even higher, offering him the whole world. Her round white ass, long legs and spread open thighs, they were everything that was good about the world for him. It was always going to be like that for Lucas. For Lucas, her sex was a wide open world.

Chapter Twenty-Six

The following morning, Lucas showed up late at the office wearing the same clothes he'd had on the day before. Susie noticed it the minute he stepped off the elevator. She found it very intriguing, but she kept it to herself.

When Miss Morrow brought Lucas his cup of coffee, she noticed it, too.

"No thank you," he told her, "I've had enough coffee. I had a late breakfast today."

Miss Morrow wasn't accustomed to being left out of the loop, but she graciously took his cup of coffee back to the little kitchen and unceremoniously dumped it down the sink. Then she consulted the main schedule planner in her computer and looked up Lucas's appointments for the day.

No breakfast meetings, she noted, and the little wheels began turning furiously in her head.

The door from Mr. Cain's office opened suddenly, and he appeared.

"Miss Morrow," he said brightly, "I'm taking the day off. Call Thomas and have him meet me downstairs." Then he walked right back out of the office and left the building.

* * *

It was a beautiful autumn day, as if the weather were made to order for lovers. Lucas called Evie from the car phone. "Get that cute ass of yours out of bed," he told her.

"How did you know I went back to bed?"

"I guessed. Look, I've taken the day off and we're coming to get you in the car. You and I are going on a little adventure."

Evie was delighted. She shot out of bed and took a quick shower. By the time the Lincoln was in front of her house, she was ready and waiting.

Thomas helped her into the car. "Good morning, Miss Donovan," he said. "Good to see you again."

Lucas was waiting for her in the back seat, a look of sheer contentment on his face, and in an uncharacteristic move, as the car started up the block he raised the partition that separated them from Thomas. They were completely alone in the back of the dark car. "Come here," he said, pulling her up close to him and giving her a quick kiss on the mouth. "I have a request."

"And what's that?"

He felt up under her skirt. She had on another pair of those incredible stockings. He felt for her panties. "Get rid of these. You won't need them today."

"You mean now?" She was instantly excited. Without so much as a protest, she slipped her hands up under her skirt and slid her panties off. "Where are we going?" she asked with glee.

"I told you already, on an adventure."

The car moved onto the highway and headed in the direction of Solisville.

"Are we going to your house?" she asked.

"No," he said, "we're going to your house."

"My house? What do you mean?"

"I thought we'd take a little plantation tour."

She laughed. "Are you serious? We're going up to the old DuMaret place?"

"Yes."

"We're going to take the tour?"

"Yes."

She thought for a moment. "Then why did I have to take my panties off?"

"Because I wanted you to be on your best behavior, Evie, after all, you're a DuMaret."

She didn't know what he was talking about, but her belly fluttered. She was incredibly excited.

Her bare thighs were beginning to sweat against the leather car seat. "It's a long ride," she hinted.

"That it is," he agreed.

"No one can see us," she tried again.

"No, no one."

Try as she might, Evie couldn't convince Lucas to fool around with her in the back of the Lincoln. She was reduced to having to make small talk with him for the duration of the trip to Solisville, but it did nothing to keep her anticipation in check. When they pulled into the drive of her old family home, she was wet between her legs. "I think I'm making a mess on the seat," she complained.

But all Lucas did was smile.

Thomas came around and opened the door for her. She slid out of the car as modestly as she could followed closely by Lucas, who took her gallantly by the arm when they were both outside.

There were several tour buses already parked in the drive along with a handful of private cars, even though half of the house hadn't undergone renovations yet and wasn't open to the public. A guard house and a little ticket booth had been erected on the front lawn. A line of people were waiting to buy tickets, and it was obvious that a busload of people were already marching through the house.

Evie looked around at everything almost as if it were a dream. It looked familiar, and yet it was decidedly different. The feeling of being home was gone. She looked to Lucas for instructions. "What are we doing next?"

He took his wallet from his back pocket and handed her some bills. "Go stand in line for a couple of tickets," he told her. "I'll wait here. And behave," he added. "Don't fool too much with your skirt. I'll have my eye on you."

With a stupid grin on her face, Evie got in the ticket line. Knowing Lucas was watching her, knowing he knew she was naked under her skirt, was making her crazy. She was horny as hell. "Next?" the ticket taker called.

"Two tickets, please. Adult," Evie said.

The ticket taker didn't recognize her. He simply sold her the two adult tickets and sent her on her way. "Next?" she heard him call again as she headed back toward Lucas.

"Well, I've got the tickets, now what? Are we really taking this tour?"

"Yes, but not right away. It's free to explore the grounds and they're really beautiful here, very well maintained."

No, Evie was thinking, he's not serious… "I hope we're not going to get arrested, Lucas."

"I hope not," he agreed.

"Lucas, you're not thinking what I think you're thinking, are you?"

"That depends, what do you think I'm thinking?"

"I don't know, maybe about having sex out there beneath the trees?"

"Well, as much as I do tend to think about that," he said, putting his arm around her affectionately, "that wasn't was I was thinking of just now. I really was just thinking about taking a look at the grounds, remembering things we did there together."

Evie was touched. "That's sweet," she whispered.

"I want to stroll around here like regular people, have my arm around you and tell you some things."

"What kinds of things?"

"All kinds of tings."

"Well, why did I need to have my panties off then?" she asked.

"Just part of the adventure, part of my gift to you today. I know how much you love to feel sexy, I know how much you love to think there's sex around every corner, and there will be, at least around one of these corners, I'm not sure which one. But the anticipation is half of it, isn't it?"

"Lucas, you're crazy. But I like you."

"I like you, too. And Evie," he added, "I want to apologize. You didn't really let me say it last night, but I really am sorry, and there are some things about myself I want to explain."

They strolled together, sometimes arm in arm, sometimes holding hands, and Lucas told Evie a bit of the story of his life, about Corinna Cain and his less than auspicious beginnings, about his jobs, his life at Miss Willie's, and then the world that awaited him when he went to work for Lucille.

Evie was okay with all of it, and Lucas saw that he'd been foolish to worry about her. He regretted that he'd allowed it to come between them for so long.

"The way you lived in Bywater," she said. "Did my dad have a life like that, too?"

"His mom made a mistake, Evie. It was bad judgment. I don't think she was a whore."

"Is that how you think of your mother?"

"Yes, sometimes. Mostly, I try not to think of her at all."

"That's sad. I love thinking about my mother. Even though she left me, too, I really wish I could have known her."

"Well, I think I can help," Lucas said. "We can start by living life the way she did, the way both your parents did before everything fell apart on them."

"Is that what this is about?"

"That's what this is about," he admitted. "We're going to make up for lost time, and we're going to seize the world by the horns, starting today."

It suddenly became clear to Evie what Lucas was trying to tell her. They were in it together, the big adventure.

"I'll try not to work my life away," he promised. "I'll try to make more time for you than your father had running Donovan & Company. I don't know if that's possible, but if it isn't, I'll quit. It's just a job in the long run. I've been working since I was ten-years-old. I'm willing to try the love thing if you are."

Evie didn't know if she should believe him. "Are your serious?"

"I'm serious. I love you, Evie. I always have. I'm sorry I had to make everything so complicated. I'm sorry I ever listened to your father. I'm sorry I underestimated you."

They walked up the old porch steps and gave the docent their tickets.

In the foyer, they stopped and waited for the line to move. There was a velvet cord roping off the stairway. The upper floor wasn't open to the public yet.

When the line moved on to the next room, Evie held back. "Come on," she said, "let's do it." Together they slipped over the rope and hurried upstairs. "I have a feeling," she added quietly, "that this is one of those corners sex is waiting around."

The upstairs was quiet and dark. Most of the rooms were in various stages of reconstruction. She thought first of her old bedroom, but then thought better of it. "Let's go where the ghosts hang out," she suggested.

Lucas followed her to the old master suite. The renovations in that room were nearly complete and it took Evie's breath away. "Wow," she sighed. "Do you think my ancestors really lived like this? It's pretty impressive, isn't it?"

Lucas had to admit he was impressed. "So there are ghosts here?" he asked.

"I think so. My mother died here, so did my dad. God only knows how many of the others died in their sleep here as well." The old floor boards creaked and they were afraid of giving themselves away. "It's kind of creepy, huh?"

"A little. I can see why this house was a lot to live with. It comes with so many other people attached. Still…"

"What is it?" she whispered.

"It might be nice to consummate our vows in the old DuMaret marriage bed."

"I thought you didn't think about marriage, Lucas?"

"I didn't used to."

She suddenly felt very excited. She pushed him down on the bed and unzipped his fly. "You better get hard right this minute," she warned him quietly, "because I sure don't want to get caught." She retrieved his cock from inside his briefs and worked it out through his open fly.

The touch of her hands on him made him get hard instantly.

Evie mounted him, placing the head of his cock at the opening of her hole and lowering herself down on it. They both gasped, but the need for absolute silence was imperative.

She rocked herself around on him gently, trying not to shake the creaky old bed. She felt his cock probe up into her all the way, and the look of sheer desire on his face as he tried so hard not to make a sound was enough to make her want to come.

She leaned down close to him, letting her hole ride him a little, up and down, up and down... "Lucas," she whispered as softly as she could, "I love you. Thank you for this."

"You're welcome," he said, holding her close to him, thrusting up into her as she gently rode him. "I love you, too, Evie."

As quietly as they could, they made love like that, on the old DuMaret marriage bed, with that old DuMaret spirit.

Evie knew that her ancestors, and the whole town of Solisville, would be scandalized by this, but she'd finally figured out how to take her own chances. She felt like a DuMaret at last, living life for herself and making her own decisions, regardless of what everyone expected. She rocked herself harder on Lucas, helping him come. "Where's the next corner?" she whispered, leaning down close to him and kissing his mouth again.